D0956043

THE
MINUS-
ONE
CLUB

PRAISE FOR KEKLA MAGOON

NAACP Image Award Winner
Printz Honor Winner
National Book Award Finalist
Margaret A. Edwards Award Winner
Boston Globe–Horn Book Award Winner
John Steptoe New Talent Award Winner
Coretta Scott King Honoree
Walter Award Honoree

"Malcolm inspired me with his eloquence, his wisdom, and his thirst for truth and righteousness. This powerful, page-turning story tells us how he discovered these qualities within himself."
—Muhammad Ali on *X: A Novel*

"Brilliantly crafted, heart-wrenching, and unforgettable."
—Laurie Halse Anderson, *New York Times*–bestselling author of *Speak* on *How It Went Down*

★ "This gritty, emotional tale will leave readers gutted and compelled to stand against flawed systems."
—*Publishers Weekly*, starred review for *Light It Up*

ALSO BY KEKLA MAGOON

The Rock and the River

37 Things I Love (in No Particular Order)

Fire in the Streets

How It Went Down

X: A Novel

Light It Up

*Revolution in Our Time: The Black Panther
Party's Promise to the People*

THE MINUS-ONE CLUB

Kekla Magoon

Henry Holt and Company
New York

Henry Holt and Company, *Publishers since 1866*
Henry Holt® is a registered trademark of Macmillan Publishing Group, LLC
120 Broadway, New York, NY 10271 • fiercereads.com

Our books may be purchased in bulk for promotional, educational, or business use. Please
contact your local bookseller or the Macmillan Corporate and Premium Sales Department
at (800) 221-7945 ext. 5442 or by email at MacmillanSpecialMarkets@macmillan.com.

Library of Congress Control Number: 2022916284

First edition, 2023
Book design by Samira Iravani
Printed in the United States of America.

ISBN 978-1-250-80620-8 (hardcover)
10 9 8 7 6 5 4 3 2 1

for Jack

IT BEGINS

The room is as cold as a secret, but nowhere near as dark. I see their faces clearly, and I recognize them, and it's strange because they're all looking directly at me, too, as the door closes firmly behind me.

It smells like hunks of clay in here. I know the smell because I took an art class in this room last semester. It's a damp, earthy, springing aroma that adds to the weirdness of things.

The others are sitting at a round tabletop near the chalk-board. It's the table where the art teacher, Ms. Hanover, lays out samples during class. I've never seen it empty of artwork before.

It's not totally empty now. In the middle of the paint-flecked wooden surface stands a deck of cards and a small brown box. And everyone's hands, resting loosely around the edges.

There are four people seated, plus two empty chairs. They are all juniors and seniors.

Janna Collins, co-captain of the Spirit dance team, holds out one hand, palm up, indicating that I should join them. Her hair hangs perfectly, a dark curtain around her face. No bangs, just a part down the middle like one of those seventies pop singers my sister got really into right before she went off to college. Totally randomly, I picture Janna's would-be album cover—featuring pom-poms and a really short flouncy skirt. My sister's voice pops into my head: *She's got the looks all right, but can she sing?*

I shake off the thought and slide into the chair Janna indicated, which is next to Simon Rogers. He's a year ahead of me, a junior. I don't know him well at all. He's on the chess team or math league or something geeky like that, and he was voted junior class treasurer, so he must have a lot of friends.

The others are Celia Berman and Patrick O'Halloran. Celia's a junior, and that's all I know, although she has clay under her fingernails and brown stains on the tips of her fingers so maybe she's in art class, which tells me she's not a lost cause. Patrick's a senior. He plays football and runs track or cross-country or something, I think. He's a big deal in the school sports world, which is far on the other side of what I know.

They all look at me. Celia picks at the remnants of clay on her hands. Simon drums his fingers on the table. Patrick remains perfectly still, hands folded. Maybe it's an athlete thing. Janna gazes at me, quiet and steady, and the whole thing gets weirder by the second.

"Hi," I say.

No one answers.

All told, this is one of the more surreal things that's happened to me this week. Which is saying something.

The deck of playing cards on the table is the traditional kind, with the familiar red design on the back. My eyes stray to it, over and over, and away from everything—everyone—else.

The small brown box is similar to the file on our kitchen counter where my mom is supposed to keep her recipes neatly organized and printed on index cards. Really, most of them are in a Tupperware case on the middle shelf of the pantry, torn loose leaf out of magazines or scrawled on scraps of paper where she or my sister jotted something down while watching TV or surfing the internet.

I'm scared to speak again, into the silence. It isn't really silent, though, because outside the art room door, I can hear lockers slamming and kids talking and sneakers squeaking and the after-school bell ringing for reasons I've never understood. Does it ring every forty-two minutes all night long?

I reach into my pocket and pull out the index card I found in my locker this morning, with its cryptic message. I read it again, for the thousandth time, fold and unfold it. Try to remind myself that I was summoned here, and there must be a purpose. Plus, they all outrank me by like a dozen rungs, popularity wise. So I keep my mouth shut and sit and wait and try not to think too hard about things like pickup trucks and funerals.

The door blasts open, bringing a fresh wave of outside noise. "I'm so sorry, guys. So sorry. I got held up after class. I mean, geez, once Mrs. Markey gets on a roll there's just no stopping her."

My throat clogs instantly at the sound of his voice. *Oh God. Oh God.* It chokes me like a prayer, although I stopped believing in God six and a half days ago.

Matthew Rincorn tosses his gorgeous, sculpted self into the empty seat next to me. "Why is nobody talking?"

Still no one speaks. Janna reaches for the small brown box and flips it open. Sure enough. Index cards. A very thin stack.

"Geez, you guys," Matt says. "Are you trying to freak him out?"

"It's a ceremony, Matthew," Janna says super seriously. "Get with the program."

"You sadistic freaks," Matt says. Simon and Celia start to laugh.

Matt touches my shoulder. Actually touches me. I get goose-bumps all over. "Hi, Kermit," he says. "Welcome to the Minus-One Club."

SEVEN HOURS EARLIER

There's something abnormal about how normal everything is. The noise in the hallway is the same as always, annoying and constant and full of people laughing and sparring and going over algebra notes, as if there isn't a cloud in the sky. There's still a stain that looks vaguely like Cheez Whiz crusted on the linoleum at the base of my locker. My locker still opens with the same three-digit number; my fingers do it without me even having to think about it. The guy with the locker next to mine—Stew—still smells like falafel and mint.

I've already resigned myself to the fact that today is going to suck. On the upside, it would be hard for any day to suck as bad as every single day of the past week of my life. Logic suggests I should be on an upswing.

I fiddle in my locker longer than necessary. If I leave now, I'll be ten minutes early for first period. Usually I'm racing along with the last-minute crush. I've never been early to school. But it beats another day holed up in the house, losing all sense of time and listening to Mom cry.

Here's how it happened.

Saturday night: Terrible awful no good very bad car crash.

Sunday: House phone rings in the wee hours, pulls me to the

surface of a dream in which Tom Holland is doing unspeakable things to me with his mouth. I'm pissed at the interruption. Then Mom starts screaming really, really loud, this harsh, blood-curdling noise, and I pee myself in my half sleep because I know something hideous has happened.

Monday: A mess of hollow noise.

Tuesday: Sitting in the funeral home lobby, wanting nothing but to talk to my sister, who I've barely talked to in half a month and will never talk to again.

Wednesday: Viewings. Family in from out of town, taking my face in their clammy hands.

Thursday: Graveside. *Damn.* Throw a rose. *God damn it.*

Friday: How many times can you hear the words *I'm sorry* before your mind begins to implode?

Saturday: Watch TV under the covers in the den. All day. Mom comes in every half hour to kiss me and I suppose to make sure an intoxicated pickup truck driver hasn't crossed a double yellow line and smashed my Toyota Corolla into the two-foot-thick trunk of an oak tree, causing my instantaneous death.

Sunday: TV again. No tears. Tears would be too simple.

Monday: Today. My first day back at school since IT happened.

HOLDING UP

Alex comes up to my locker as usual. He squeezes between me and Stew and launches into the laundry list of everything I've missed in the past week, school gossip wise. "Hey, I'm really glad you're back," he goes. "I've been having these weird conversations with Cindy and it's going pretty well, I mean, weird, but pretty good, right? And I wonder what you think, you know, I mean about me asking her out and everything, but then of course there's Crystal who's always standing right there with her, giving me the stink eye, and maybe you could fend her off this time while I talk to Cindy, and see if she, you know . . ."

I stare into the green metal abyss, at the fishhooks that are supposed to be holding up my jacket, which I'm still wearing. I shrug out of it and hang it inside.

"Hey, man," Alex says. "How you holding up?"

I slam my locker. "What does that even mean?" People keep saying it to me and I don't know how to respond.

Alex flinches backward, bumping into Stew, who doesn't seem to notice. "I don't know," he says. "It's just what you say."

"Sorry," I mutter. I pinch the bridge of my nose as if it's going to help something.

"It's okay," he says.

"Maybe I should just go back home."

Alex groans. "No. You have to stay, man. I need you. This whole thing with Cindy is killing me. Oh, crap. I shouldn't say things like 'killing me,' huh? I'm such a dick. I'm really sorry."

"It's fine."

"I feel really bad now."

"Don't. It's not like what you say is gonna make it worse."

He runs his hand through his hair. "Well, just give me a little time, and I'm sure I can come up with something. You know I can't keep my trap shut. I've finally perfected exactly how wide I need to open it to fit in my foot." He lifts up his leg really high.

I can't help but smile. "Finally. You nailed it. It's taken you years."

Alex settles a hand on my shoulder. "Seriously, you're like my brother," he says. "You know, so whatever I can do."

The little surge in my chest is full of things. I'm grateful, because he is a good friend, even when I'm not treating him like it. I'm pissed, because he's not my brother; I don't have a brother. I had a sister, but now I don't and the vacuum of that is everywhere.

"Okay."

We walk in silence down the hallway toward my first-period class.

"Just be normal," I tell him. "Say ridiculous crap."

He looks offended. "Why do you gotta diminish me, man? Every raindrop off this tongue is solid gold."

"You're mixing metaphors again."

"Mix Master Flash," he says. "Wikka-wikka," which is supposed to be the sound of a DJ mixing a turntable.

I roll my eyes. "You're a freak."

"Right back at ya." We slap hands and bump shoulders and then peel off our separate ways to head to class.

AFTER FIRST PERIOD

The narrow sliver of Scotch tape happens to be exactly at my eye level. It pokes out through my locker vent. Inside, there's a blur of white. Someone has stuck something in there. For no good reason, my fingers start to shake. I get my locker combo wrong and have to do it again.

A small white card, with a neatly typed message:

> You don't know us, but we know you.
> Sorry about your sister.
> As much as it sucks, we can help you.
> Art room. Today. 2:45.
> Be there.
> Or don't.
> Whatever.
> (This card is biodegradable. Crush it and flush it. Now.)

I flip the card over. The back is white, except for a small notation in the top left corner:

-1

NOW

Janna opens the wooden box and extracts a thin stack of note cards. She hands them to Patrick who hands them to Matt who hands them to me. I'm still not over the fact that Matt Rincorn knows my name. My shoulder is warm where he touched me.

I look at the cards. The top one is typed, like the one I found in my locker.

RULES

1. Tell no one else about us.
2. We never talk about *IT*.
3. Ever.
4. *Ever.*

The rest are handwritten. Six cards, total. I flip past the blank one.

MY DAD DIED IN A SAILING ACCIDENT.
THEY NEVER EVEN FOUND HIS BODY.

PATRICK O'HALLORAN

My twin sister had leukemia since we were seven. Last year,
I gave her my bone marrow. She still died.

Celia Berman

My grandpa was like my dad. He was old, but he was
my only family. He had a stroke, and now he's gone.

Simon Rogers

My mom wanted me to learn how to drive in a snowstorm. I slid
off the road and wrecked the car. She died in the accident.

Janna Collins

MY MOTHER DIED OF PANCREATIC CANCER.

MATTHEW I. RINCORN

The final card is blank. From the box, Janna pulls a blue ball-point and slides it across the table to me. Patrick pushes it the rest of the way until I can reach it.

"Are you in?" he says.

My fingers fumble around the pen like I've never held one before. I'm five years old again, and writing is new. Everything is new. The first words I ever wrote were with crayons on tracing paper, set on big fat letters my sister wrote for me to copy. There's nothing to trace now. The footsteps I've always tried to walk in are fading in front of my eyes.

I squeak out the words, one by one. It's the first time I've had to do anything but think them:

My sister was killed by a drunk driver.
Kermit Sanders

"Okay," Matt says. He takes the card out of my hands, and I dry them against my pant legs. My card goes into the pile with the other cards, and back into the box. Patrick whisks them away and they disappear into the outside pouch of his backpack.

"This meeting is hereby in session." Janna pounds her fist on the table. "What happens in the room stays in the room."

"I swear," the others intone in unison.

What's going to happen?

"Kermit," Janna scolds. "You have to swear."

"I swear."

NO-LIMIT TEXAS HOLD'EM

Simon reaches for the deck of playing cards and begins to shuffle. "Did anyone see my op-ed in the *Cryer* about getting solar panels on the cafeteria roof?"

"No one reads the school paper except for you, doofus," Janna says.

I saw the article. Should I say I saw the article?

Simon deals everyone five cards, facedown. "Y'all are a bunch of newsless know-nothings."

Celia sniffs. "Pop culture is so passé."

"Oh my God," Janna says. "Why must you be so pretentious?"

Celia sniffs again. "Because it's fun." She cracks a smile as her clay-stained hands deftly shift the order of cards in her hand.

"Why must she?" murmurs Matt. "Pot. Kettle." Janna shoots him a dirty look that morphs silly when she sticks her tongue out.

"News is not pop culture," Simon grumbles. "It's *news*."

"I read it." My voice is small in the room. "It was good."

Simon looks at me. "The game is no-limit Texas Hold'em. It's ongoing. We'll stake you a dollar up front. If you run out of pennies after that, it's your problem."

Patrick sends a tube of pennies rolling toward me. It rocks to a stop right in front of me.

One end of the penny tube is dented, giving it the tapered look of a tiny brown penis. I fold my hand around it and fight the urge to giggle.

In my head, Sheila's voice goes, *Oh my God; you're such a little perv.*

Don't I know it.

I use my nail to flick up the penny penis head—ha ha—and tear back the wrapper.

"You ever played Texas rules before?" Simon asks me.

"Just regular poker."

"Draw?"

"I guess." I know the various poker hands. Full house. Straight. Flush. I just don't always remember what order they go in.

Simon rattles off the basic rules, which include something about flops and rivers. Cards will be turned over. I've seen this on TV. It'll be okay.

"You got it?" he says.

I shuffle my cards into order by suit. "Um, which is better, a straight or a flush? I always forget that part."

"Straight's not better than anything," Matt pipes up. "That's how I remember it." Everyone but me laughs.

I want to laugh, too, but I can't. "Okay."

"Got it now?" Matt Rincorn smiles at me. At *me*. In response, my mouth does something that I hope comes across more like a smile than drooling.

Matt was hot even before he came out last year, but after that his hotness, like, quadrupled. Sexy and strong and brave. The only out gay guy in our entire high school. Quite a few schools in the area have actual GSAs and such, but not ours. We live in the

15

vortex between three megachurches, and it shows. Matt coming out made him practically a legend.

I'm not the only anything. Not the only Black guy—not even the only biracial—not the only blue belt, and nowhere near the only Christian. (If I can still call myself one since my heart lives in sin.) I'm probably not the only guy who secretly crushes on Matt Rincorn.

Turns out, I'm not even the only one with a dead sister. I glance at Celia, who's stacking an impressive amount of pennies on the table out of a plastic sandwich baggie. Everyone else does the same. The sound of pennies clicking on fake wood has an eerie rhythm, like the chorus echoing in my head.

Sheila is dead.

Sheila is dead.

Sheila.

Is.

Dead.

It sounds harsh to keep repeating it like that, but I constantly need to remind myself.

CRUSH

After club, I linger, pretending to look for something in my backpack. Really I'm watching Matt. Lean muscles under a fitted polo shirt. He dresses nicely, at least compared to most of the guys in school. I wonder if he works out, or what. He's not super buff, like Patrick, but he has really nice arms and shoulders.

"You want a ride home?" he says.

"Sure." I jump at the offer. "Oh, but I have to call my mom first." I cringe, because it makes me sound like a kindergartner. "I mean, to tell her she doesn't need to come get me." She's probably already on her way.

"Okay," Matt says. He hoists his backpack and shifts his weight to the other foot as I pull out my cell.

"Honey?" Mom's voice is anxious. "Are you okay?"

"Mom, you don't have to come get me," I tell her. "I got a ride home."

"No," she says. "I'm coming to get you."

"I'm saying you don't have to. Aren't you still home?"

"*No*," Mom declares, her voice shrill. "You do not get in anyone's car. Do I make myself clear?"

The seismic urgency in her tone shreds all hope to dust.

Tipping the phone away from my mouth, I shake my head at Matt. "No-go."

He frowns.

"I don't know what you were thinking, missing the bus," Mom says. "Now I have to come get you."

I turn away from Matt and lower my voice, as if it'll stop him from hearing. "I called, remember? You said it was okay to stay after."

"I'm coming to get you."

"Okay, Mom."

"I'm coming now."

"Okay."

"You had better be there waiting for me."

"Mom."

"Do you want to be grounded until the other side of time?"

"*Mom*. I said okay."

"I'll be there in five minutes." Which is a total lie. Home is a fifteen-minute drive away.

"Take your time," I tell her. "It's no big deal."

"I love you, sweetie," she says. "Please be safe."

"I will."

"I love you."

And . . . now she's not hanging up the phone. I can't hang up on her. I know what she's waiting for, and it's going to embarrass the shit out of me.

I cover the mouthpiece with my hand. "I love you, too," I whisper. Then I click off.

Matt's holding his backpack strap and staring at his shoes. Or mine. I can't tell.

"Sorry. I guess I don't need a ride. She's already on her way."

He probably knows I'm lying. It's not like Mom was whispering. No such thing as a soundproof cell phone.

"Next time," he says. "If she's cool with it." Yep, he knows.

"Next time," I agree. "Hey, when is the next time?"

"We meet when we feel like it." He shrugs. "Not always at school, though. You'll get the hang of it."

We walk outside, taking our time. At the curb by the pickup lane, Matt lingers like he's going to wait with me.

"You don't have to wait."

"Sure?" he says.

"Yeah. She'll be here any minute."

We look down the lane. No cars coming yet.

A spiteful, reckless little nugget of my soul speaks up. Without permission. "Actually, who cares? I'll just go with you anyway." My feet respond to the same illicit call; they tip toward the parking lot. I step off the curb, and now I'm looking up at him.

Matt grins. "You wanna be some kind of rebel?"

No. I don't know. Maybe. "Let's just go," I beg him. "Anywhere you want."

"Naw." Matt lays a hand on my shoulder. It's the third time he's touched me there. So much fuel for my fantasies. There's a warm shower in my immediate future. The minute I get home. Not to wash him off, but to . . . imagine.

"Please," I say, and maybe there's a little crack in my voice. Because maybe I don't want to see Mom right now. Maybe I don't want her to light into me about whatever is pissing her off about me. Maybe Matt Rincorn has touched me one too many times now, and with everything so close to the surface, maybe I won't be able to hide my feelings for the fifteen minutes it takes us to get home.

"Kermit, don't worry about it. There's going to be plenty of time for us to get in trouble later."

There is?

The picture rises in my mind: Matt and me together, whipping down a paved black road, windows down so the air rushes in, holding hands and laughing. It almost could have been today.

"For now, why don't you cut your mom some slack," he says. "I mean, considering what just happened. I totally get it."

From behind Matt Rincorn's wry smile, an imaginary brick wall comes flying at me. Seventy-five, eighty miles an hour. When the windshield glass shatters, the pieces turn white, like his teeth.

That's right, little bro, Sheila's voice whispers in my head. *I ruined everything.*

STRANGER DANGER (VEHICULAR EDITION)

"I don't want you riding with strangers," Mom says. As if this is going to undo the past week somehow.

"The taxi driver. The limo driver. Two limo drivers, actually." I tick them off on my fingers. All the strangers I've ridden with in the past week. "My bus driver. Uncle Justin."

"Uncle Justin's not a stranger."

"He drives like an imbecile. Even I drive better than he does."

"You don't drive," she snaps.

"That's the point." Sheesh. Usually Mom has a sense of humor. Especially about Uncle Justin.

"I don't want you riding with anyone but me and Dad," Mom says.

I cross my arms. "Great. I'll be seventy years old and my hundred-year-old mother will be driving me around town."

"By then, you can drive me around. It's just for now," she adds.

"For now?" I echo.

"For the foreseeable future."

"I can foresee myself at seventy," I tell her. Which is a lie. I can foresee myself in lit class tomorrow, and that's about it. On the other hand, I can foresee Sheila as a sophomore, junior, senior in college, which is a picture I have to dismantle.

"It's just for now," Mom repeats.

"Right. Because you're going to get over it?"

Mom grips the wheel so tight her knuckles turn actual white. She rolls her lips into a thin line.

"Sorry," I mumble.

She says nothing the rest of the way home.

HAIR CLIPS AND HEARTBREAKERS

In the dream, we're at a picnic. Just the two of us—Sheila and me. This never happened in real life, but it feels real enough. She has her hair down and streaming in the wind, wild and lovely and swirling in her face the way she hates but that looks really awesome, especially to me with my forever quarter-inch buzz cut. I'm holding her hair clips hostage and jumping up and down. "Damn it, Kermie," she says. "Freaking give them to me."

"No." I hold them behind my back. "Pick a hand."

Clearly, I'm in my magic phase. I can't see myself in the dream, but I must be nine or ten.

The blanket beneath us is Sheila's childhood bedspread, covered with cartoon turtles who apparently dance. She got rid of it when she went into high school and wanted to act all grown-up, so it ended up in a wad in the basement. Now the turtles dance beneath us, slow smooth steps that are meant to be a samba.

My own bedspread was of a similar fashion, except greener instead of purplish, with frogs instead of turtles. The irony was not lost on me or Sheila. Only Mom, who picked them out.

"Gimme!" Sheila dives at me, but misses. Her hair becomes

a swirling nest for dancing frogs and turtles. She sits up and glares at me.

I sing at her, still jumping: "You're gonna be a heartbreaker."

Uncle Justin used to say that about her. "Your sister's gonna be a heartbreaker. Just like your mom was at that age. All the boys were after her." Ew, gross. Who wants to think about Mom as a teenager with boys?

"I can make them reappear," I shout.

"Give them back."

"Ready? One, two . . ." I pump my fist. "Three!" My hand opens as if to throw the hair clips at her, but they've disappeared.

Not disappeared—reappeared, on the sides and top of Sheila's head, holding back her hair in exactly the way she likes.

Sheila smiles at me. "Kermie, how did you do that?"

Maybe I smile, or maybe the world simply widens, like a grin. "Magic."

WAFFLES

I sigh myself awake.

Sheila used to like to rub her hands on the top of my head. Especially after a haircut. It drove me absolutely mad.

Our hair is different. Was. Her hair is long and soft and wavy. Was. Her hair was darker than mine, too, at least a little. That must be why she liked touching mine, which was textured instead of smooth. Close-cropped instead of long.

I would let her touch my head a thousand times a day, or kiss my cheeks, if she could only be not-dead again.

My door creaks open. "Morning, sweetie."

Mom shovels folded laundry out of the basket in the door-way and onto my rug. It softly plops in little piles that I won't ever put away, even though Mom is right now saying, "Put these away, okay?"

Mom doing laundry is far too normal. How is it that all the normal stuff just keeps happening?

And how does she always know exactly when I'm going to wake up? It's creepy. Or maybe I woke up because I sensed her there.

Things to not ponder as I roll over and snuggle deeper. I had a good dream. Maybe I can get another.

"Are you getting up?" Mom says. "I made waffles."

"I don't like waffles."

Her frown is audible. "You love waffles."

She's wrong. "Go away."

"The first batch is already cold," she says. "When will you be down? Should I unplug the waffle iron?"

"Sounds like a safe bet to me."

"Sweetie."

"*Go away*. Why are you in here? Can't you see I'm sleeping?"

"You need clean clothes."

"Not really."

"Fine. Be dirty."

The door creaks shut.

THEN: WAFFLE MONSTER (EIGHT YEARS AGO)

"**Why do we** have to have waffles *again*?" I moan, glaring at the pile.

"Because they're delicious," Sheila says, forking heart-shaped waffles onto her plate. One. Two. Three. The fourth one is mine, but it sits there cooling while I protest.

"I want pancakes," I declare, crossing my arms.

"Too bad," Mom says, returning to the kitchen. "We can have pancakes next weekend."

The saving grace on the table is the giant mound of crispy bacon. I grab most of it in a double handful, leaving the waffles untouched.

"Excuse you, sir." Mom's voice carries from the kitchen. "Leave some bacon for the rest of us." How did she know?

"Grrr," I mutter, returning some of the bacon.

Sheila laughs, dumping a lake of syrup on her waffle hoard. "Did you actually *grrr* at me?"

"GRRR." It's not like waffles are *so* bad, but once you've made a stand it's hard to back down. "People should know by now not to make me eat waffles."

"People should be grateful there is food on the table," Mom calls. "Eat it or don't. Up to you."

"I didn't know you don't like waffles," Sheila says around a mouthful. "You ate them last week and didn't say anything."

My *grrr* face returns. "Maybe there are lots of things you don't know about me." In the moment, I don't know where it comes from, to say that, but the truth of it is as deep as my bones.

"Maybe there are lots of things you don't know about me, too," Sheila whispers. "Like, did you know"—she takes the point of one of the waffle hearts between her teeth, letting it hang down over her chin, dripping syrup everywhere—"I'm a waffle monster?" She holds two pieces of bacon on either side of her nose like a mustache. Then she jams them into the corners of her mouth, behind the waffle, and lunges across the table toward me, her long arms extended and tickling until I'm shrieking with laughter and the table is dribbled with syrup that Mom will make us wipe up in a minute. But it's worth it.

NOW: TO BE CLEAR

Evidently, Mom didn't unplug the waffle iron. At least not right away. She made a whole batch of palm-sized heart-shaped waffles, joined by their angles in clover configurations of four. They're stacked up and sitting there on the counter, under a curl of paper towels.

"Pop them in the toaster," she says. She's sitting at the kitchen table, which is full of a pile of note cards she is writing.

I carry the plate across the kitchen, tip the mountain of waffles straight into the trash bin.

Mom stares at me. I take a carton of orange juice and a summer sausage out of the fridge.

"It's Sheila who liked waffles." This is only to hurt Mom. No other reason.

I'm going back to bed.

BACK TO THE GRIND

It's Monday again, somehow. I managed to sleep away the weekend, but even that wasn't enough. By lunchtime, I'm dragging myself through the halls, praying for the day to come to an end. But clearly God has marked himself "on hiatus" and isn't even checking his DMs.

My parents went to church yesterday, like usual. I don't know how they can stand it. All the gushing and cooing and "she's in a better place." Fuck that.

They didn't fight me on it, which was amazing. Perhaps I'm suspended in some kind of grace period, where I get away with things that would normally be unacceptable. In my family, getting out of going to church is harder than getting out of going to school.

The last straw for me fell a while ago, I've just been unable to admit it. Stuck in a pattern of obedience that I don't know how to break. And the relief I feel now comes with a hefty side helping of shame. Yesterday, for a few minutes there, I was *happy*. Even in spite of the ad jingle playing in the back of my mind: *This carefree Sunday morning made possible by the death of Sheila Sanders.*

The smell of mystery meat from the cafeteria spikes my

existing nausea. I go toward the à la carte line and grab a couple of dinner rolls and a tub of ice cream. Who needs real food when you have gnawing guilt to sustain you?

My phone lights up with a text message. It's from Simon. *After school*, he writes. *Be ready.*

PERSONAL ESCORT

Matt Rincorn meets me at my locker after school. "Hey, Kermit."

"Hey. Ouch, what happened?" He has a bruise on his neck, high up in the triangle between his ear and jaw.

He touches the spot. "Fuck gym class, amirite?"

"Looks painful."

Matt shrugs. "No more than anything else. You ready to do this thing?"

"I guess. What's the thing?"

"Just a thing we do," he says.

He's standing awfully near me, and so I lose my words. But it's not even awkward. We wait the ten minutes until the buses have left, then walk down the empty hallways side by side. I want to kick myself. Snap out of it. Maybe it's all been a dream. One long terrible dream, finally blended into this awesome moment which will of course be the time when my alarm clock goes off. Any second now.

"You like laser tag?" Matt says, shattering the potential dream space.

"What?"

"Laser tag. What are your feelings on the subject?"

"I've never played."

"Bullshit. Everyone plays. You've never played?"

"No."

"Oh, Kermit." He shakes his head. "We have to rectify this travesty immediately."

"I'm game."

"You better be. Laser tag is about the greatest thing ever. It's like a real live video game." Matt stops short. He grabs my arm and clutches at his heart with the other hand. "Hold the phone. You do play video games, don't you?"

"Of course."

"Oh good."

I'm mildly offended. "I have a PS4 and Switch. What do you take me for?"

"Well, I took you for cool," he says. "But then I found out you're a laser tag virgin, so I have to recalibrate."

"Sorry to cause you heart palpitations." I'm not sorry at all actually. He's been causing them in me for months now, from a distance. Revenge is sweet.

"No, no," he says. "That would have been full-fledged cardiac arrest."

"I would have just told you I time-traveled here from the 1960s. You know, to spare you death. And me embarrassment."

He makes a Y with his hand and trembles it. "Psychedelic."

"I think that's the seventies."

"Whatevs."

"That's the nineties."

We laugh.

"So you're gonna pop my laser-tag cherry?" I can't believe I just said that out loud.

"Yes," Matt says, linking our arms. "Your life is never going to be the same." He pulls me toward him until we're side by side, arms looped at the elbows. His arm hair tickles mine and our biceps align. It feels . . . I tug my arm to free it.

"I'm sorry," Matt gasps, instantly unlinking our arms. He backs away, toward the wall, like he's afraid of me all of a sudden. "I didn't mean . . . Does it bother you to have the gay guy right next to you?"

Bother me? I want to laugh. Except it's so the opposite of funny. "No."

He bumps into the cinder blocks. "Sorry," he repeats. "I don't know what . . ." His voice trails off. He glances left and right as if someone's going to see us. But the hall is empty.

When he touched me, for a second there, it didn't feel scary or anything. All the things I worry about, all the ways I'm careful disappeared. It was just . . . nice. Strange as it feels now, I take two steps closer to him. "I'm not like that."

"Not like what?"

"Afraid of people being, you know . . ."

"Gay?"

"Yeah." I wish it wasn't such a hard word to say. That's ridiculous.

STORAGE CLOSET ROULETTE

Matt bangs on the door of the storage closet in the A loop. Nothing happens.

"Dang. I always forget which hall it is," Matt says. He pulls out his phone and dashes off a text. The response is instantaneous but makes him roll his eyes.

The school is shaped like a clover leaf, with four identical loops of classrooms jutting out from the central foyer where the library is located. Down the "stem" is the cafeteria, auditorium, and gym.

"Celia says it's the storage room in C loop," Matt reports. "My bad."

"All good."

We walk back to the center and veer out into C loop. Matt pounds on the door again. Nothing.

"You have to be kidding me." He texts two words that are . . . not kind. Celia responds with a row of ROFL emojis.

"Shit. She'll never let me live this down."

"What are we doing?" I ask.

"Walking to D loop, apparently," Matt says. "Where hopefully there will be no witnesses when I kill her." He pounds one fist into the other palm and makes a roaring sound, but his grumbling is entirely good-natured.

"I didn't see anything," I report.

Matt grins.

PADDLES AND BRACKETS

We don't even have to knock. The door is ajar and the whole Minus-One Club is waiting in the D-loop storage room when we get there. The room is larger than I'd have expected, nearly the size of a classroom, jam-packed with extra desks, whiteboards, and random AV equipment, and at the center of it all, an open Ping-Pong table.

"I know you love to mess with me," Matt says by way of greeting. "But why would you do that to poor Kermit, here?"

"The walking really took it out of me," I agree, though the truth is I'm more energized than I've felt all day.

Janna grins and chucks Matt on the shoulder. "This is what we get for designating Matt as Kermit's guide."

Celia waves a Ping-Pong paddle at me. "Come on, Kermit, you get first game."

"And pick of your opponent," Patrick adds. "With no advance commentary on our respective skills."

Janna writes everyone's initials on one of the whiteboards for scorekeeping.

"I choose Mister No Sense of Direction," I declare. "I can use that kind of confusion to my advantage."

"Ooooohh." Patrick, Janna, and Simon all groan an "oh snap" groan in unison. Celia busts out laughing.

Matt shakes his head. "And to think you all were worried. Kermit here is going to fit in just fine." He grabs a paddle and points it at me. "You're on."

Perhaps I failed to mention: My dad played on his college Ping-Pong intramural team. We have a Ping-Pong table in our basement. I've got this.

BEING GREEN

Mom happens to be working a full day today, so I never bothered to text her that I was going to stay after school. I want the ride home that Matt offered me a week ago. What Mom doesn't know won't hurt her, right?

We go to Matt's car, a small sporty thing that looks fairly expensive to me, but I don't really know much about cars.

"I've always wondered," he says, "how you ended up with a name like Kermit."

Always?

"It's a family name," I mumble. "From way before the Muppets were a thing."

He grins. "You must take a lot of flak for that."

"Not as much as you'd think." Actually, hardly anyone has ever made fun of my name. I figure they have too much respect for Kermit the Frog to diminish him like that. By comparing me to him, or using him as a slur.

"Oh." Matt seems, I don't know, disappointed.

"It still ain't easy, being me," I say.

He grins again. I could fall into that smile, I think. But I pull myself back from thoughts like that. Like I always do.

JUST US

Matt pulls into my driveway. "Sometimes Patrick and I get together and hang out on the weekends," he says. "Or Simon and I. You know, as guys."

"Okay."

"So you and I can do that sometimes. If you want to."

If? "Yeah, okay."

"Yeah?" He taps his thumb on the wheel and nods. "Great. I'll text you and let you know what's up. This weekend?"

"Sure." I hop out of the car.

"Laser tag?" he calls through the open window.

"Naturally." I toss it over my shoulder, playing it casual as I head up the walk. Can't let him see the size of my smile.

GRIEVING FOR DUMMIES

I take the half flight of stairs to the den with two leaps. Mom hates when I do that, but she's not— Oops. Dad *is* home early, and is reading in the den. I pivot backward, hoping to escape before he notices me.

"Kermit," Dad calls.

No such luck. I slink through the doorway. "Yeah?"

"Come in."

The den is supposedly Dad's man cave, although it still looks pretty much like Mom in here. Except for the flat screen and all the architecture books and one weird poster of the Blues Brothers, it basically matches the decor of the rest of the house.

Dad's not even a man cave kind of guy, actually. For the first time, I wonder if Mom's really just teasing him when she says things like, "Off to the man cave?"

This is the kind of revelation I would normally discuss with Sheila.

I take only one step farther, inexplicably annoyed. "What do you want?"

"Come all the way in." Dad's sitting in the corner of the

couch, a book tented over his knee. He pats the couch beside him. "I just wanted to say hi. You don't have to bite my head off."

Maybe I do. "Sorry." I go over and sit, not where he patted, but two cushions away.

Dad sighs. "So . . ."

"So?"

"How was your day?"

"It sucked."

"Anything in particular?"

"Just the usual amount of suckage."

"How is it being back at school?"

I think about Matt, nodding to me across the cafeteria, touching my shoulder, grinning at me over the Ping-Pong table, driving me home. "Not too bad. Kinda normal, actually." Better than normal. But I'm ashamed of thinking it.

I scoot closer to Dad. Inch by inch, as if I can do it without him noticing. He puts his arm around me. The jig is up, so I go ahead and lean on his shoulder because, if not now, when? The book on his knee is titled *Grieving with Your Child*.

"I bet everything in that book is super cheesy."

Dad laughs. "Kinda." He squeezes my shoulder. "I don't know. Maybe it helps people."

Dad turns to books for everything. The books on the wall that aren't about architecture are mostly how-to books. He has half a shelf of For Dummies titles alone. He loves to tell a story about Sheila when she was little, around the time that I was born and she was learning to read. Apparently she found Dad's Dummies library and said to him, "You don't seem like such a dummy." He loved to tell that story. I wonder if he'll tell it anymore now.

"Don't they make a *Grieving for Dummies*?" I ask him. "That's what we really need."

Dad laughs. I feel it rumble through his chest and stomach. Then he squeezes me tighter and his body continues to shake behind mine and I know that he's crying.

Dad never used to cry. Now he cries all the time. It's one of many ways the world is tilted.

I wonder if they make a book called *Grieving with Your Parents*. I wouldn't buy it or anything, but I might sneak into the library and put it inside an encyclopedia and pretend to be researching rodent life or something and secretly read it. So I would know what to do when this happens. Should I leave? Should I stay? Should I say something that might make him feel better? What if it makes him feel worse?

"I didn't mean to say that," I tell him. I want to say *I'm sorry*, but I hate those words now.

"Don't ever," Dad sobs, "stop saying things because of me."

I let him hug me against his chest for a minute longer before I pull away.

"If you want to talk, we're here for you," Dad says. Tear tracks glisten like silver against the dark brown of his cheeks. "I don't want us to become one of those families where no one talks to each other."

Please. I scrunch my face at him. "How likely does that seem to you?" No one talks more than my parents.

Dad laughs. He doesn't wipe away the tear tracks, though I really want him to.

"You're just like your sister. Always sarcastic."

"I'm not like her at all." I slide off the couch. Away from him. "Don't say that ever again."

"Kerm?" Dad says. "Hang on a second."

But I can't go back to him. Not right now. Sometimes it feels like when they look at me, they are looking for her. And that isn't fair. It isn't fair at all.

TKD

Dad reminds me it's Tae Kwon Do night. Apparently this is why he came home early.

"You can't skip it forever," he says, hauling me out of the loveseat recliner where I'm immersed in *Star Trek* reruns. He might be talking about more than Tae Kwon Do. I also skipped youth group yesterday for the third week in a row. Not to mention church itself.

Dad drives me to the Dojang for my training. Usually Alex's mom picks us both up and brings us, since my house is on her way home from work and their house is closer to the Dojang.

"Seriously?" We're walking out to the car. "Not even other parents? How long is this going to last?" Asking makes me feel cold, even though I genuinely want to know.

"Let's give your mom this one, okay?" Dad says. "It's the least we can do."

"Whatever." I toss myself into the passenger seat, wondering what that turn of phrase even means in this context. What would be the most we can do? Turn back time?

THEN: PUNCHING THINGS (FOUR YEARS AGO)

I pound the doorframe with my fist, crossing into my sister's bedroom. "We really need our own TV," I tell her. A minute ago, Mom commandeered the TV for some C-SPAN coverage she apparently couldn't live without, which means no video games for the rest of the afternoon.

"No kidding." Sheila lies with her feet up the wall over her headboard.

"What are you doing?"

"Drying my toenails."

"Yeoman's work." I flop down on the end of the bed, propping my feet on the footboard so our heads are aligned in the middle.

"Don't knock it till you've tried it," she says. "I have a nice royal blue with sparkles that would really bring out your foot veins."

"Ew," I say, pretending I hate the idea.

"Don't get all boys-rule-girls-drool on me, okay? I've trained you better than that."

"Boys can paint their toenails if they want to," I intone

obediently. Sheila's budding feminism takes the form of a lot of lectures about gender expectations. "But I don't want to."

Ideas are all well and good, but she doesn't know what it's like to be a guy. Especially in middle school, when everyone is all about who has chin hair and who has muscles and who's had their growth spurt, which I haven't.

"That's okay," she says. "For now."

"I don't really see blue nail polish in my future, either, sorry. It doesn't speak to my manly-but-delicate soul."

Sheila turns her head toward me. "There's a lot inside you, Kermie. 'More than meets the eye,'" she sings, mocking the theme song of the *Transformers* movie Dad made us watch over the weekend.

Her words prick upon a sensitive spot inside me. The restless, wide-awake place that keeps turning my stomach over.

"You think I'm secretly a royal-blue tractor-trailer or something? With sparkles?"

"It's a metaphor," she says. "Don't you ever feel like your inside is different than what people see on the outside?"

"Yeah." All the time. "Do you think it's because we're biracial?"

"Maybe," she says, raising her head back to center.

We stare at the ceiling.

"Stop that," Sheila says. "It's annoying."

"What?"

"Stop pounding."

"Oh." My hand was doing it of its own accord. Beating a rhythm into the mattress with the full weight of the things I'm not saying.

"You know, we had a Tae Kwon Do unit in gym class last month. I think you'd like it. Better than a video game, right?"

"Wow. We don't get to do anything that cool in gym."

"Wait for high school," she says.

NOW: KIII-YAH!

Tae Kwon Do practice isn't the worst. Dojang Master Klein looks upon me with the usual disdain. After two missed weeks and zero practice, I'm honestly a smidge rusty, which is weird.

"Shoulders down, Sanders," he says, passing me during forms. "You're too tight."

My flow all through the starting forms is off. Not like I forgot the moves—I've been doing them for years, but it's like the part of my brain that knows them and the parts of my body that do them are disconnected. Dial tone static buzzing in my ears.

The punching and kicking part is better. Each punch starts in my toes and powers through me. Every kick knocks me off-balance in a way I know how to come back from. It's comforting. It is what it's always been: both an escape from the things plaguing me and a reminder of what's inside.

We sit down in rows for final stretches. Master Klein kneels on my back to extend the stretch. "Good focus today, Sanders. Way to power through."

Power is what I don't have. But it was nice to pretend for a minute.

WE ARE NOT PARTY PEOPLE

"**You wanna go** to a party?" Alex says Friday afternoon.

"When have I ever wanted to go to a party?" I juggle my cell against my shoulder.

"Since . . . always?" he tries. Swing and a miss.

"For that matter, when have *you* ever wanted to?"

"Cindy's gonna be there."

"Ah." My brain screams *no*.

"Please, bro."

No. "I don't know."

"Please. You don't have to enjoy it or anything. You can stand in the corner and be sad and stuff."

"Wow. You paint a compelling picture."

"I heard her talking to Crystal and planning how they're gonna get drunk tonight," Alex says.

"It's a drinking party?" Double no.

"Crap . . . uh . . . yeah."

Didn't mean to let that little tidbit slip, there, did ya, buddy? "We don't drink," I remind him.

"Yeah, but Cindy does, and what if she needs, like, a knight in shining armor, you know? What if this is my shot?"

"Do you really want it to happen that way?" I want to kick

myself for sounding like such a pompous stick-in-the-mud jackass.

"I pretty much just want it to happen," Alex says. I imagine Matt, putting his hand on my shoulder, and all of the things I might want to do if he landed, drunk, in my lap.

"I actually can't go with you. I'm not allowed to ride anywhere."

"Let's meet at Rallyburger," he says. "We can walk from there. I mapped it."

Damn.

"Please," he says. I've known him a long time, so I know how bad he wants this. His crush on Cindy isn't going anywhere any-time soon, and the fact of the matter is that I owe him, because I don't know how I would've gotten through Sheila's funeral if he hadn't been right there beside me, being a general goofball and making me feel like things might actually be okay somehow.

"I have to be home by eleven."

"Yessss," Alex exclaims. "You totally will be."

RALLYBURGER RENDEZVOUS

"Call me when you're ready," Mom says in the Rallyburger parking lot. "Otherwise I'll be back at eleven."

"Okay." I leap out of the car and slam the door.

As is usual at seven thirty on a Friday night, Rallyburger is hopping with kids from school. I weave among table after table of classmates and acquaintances. Is it me, or do people glance away more than usual as I pass? Are they laughing extra hard so they can throw their heads back and avoid eye contact?

Alex is sitting all the way in back at a table for four, with our friends Bill and Scott.

"We're only here for a minute. Kerm and I have something we need to do," Alex is telling the others. He turns to me. "Hey, bud." He pushes out my chair with his foot.

I flop down across from him. "Hey."

Alex is the only one looking at me. Bill and Scott become suddenly very interested in their fries.

"Hey," I repeat.

"Hey," they mumble, mouths full. Then no one says anything for about a full minute.

"Geez, you guys. Who died?" I joke. I'm the only one who laughs. Bill blushes redder than the sunset. Scott just chews and stares.

Alex pushes his plate toward me. "I saved you half of my burger."

I scarf it in record time. Three and a half bites. Fries, straight down the hatch like sailors into a submarine.

"You ready?" Alex throws eight bucks onto the table.

I swig water, spitting back the ice cubes. "Yep."

"Bye, guys," we say.

"Bye." Bill and Scott seem relieved that we're going.

We weave back through the tables, headed for the parking lot. It's not my imagination. People avert their eyes. People who were not invited to Steve Burns's party, and who will be stuck at Rallyburger for the next three hours, are trying to make it seem like the cool place to be. A group that usually includes Alex and me. Come to think of it, why did we get invited to Steve Burns's party?

Alex seems to know where he's going. I follow.

"Well, that was weird."

"They don't know what to say. We were talking about it before you got there."

"Great. So everyone is talking about me?"

"Not everyone. Well, kinda."

"Great."

"People feel bad."

"Good for them."

"It'll be fine."

Right. I'm sure that *fine* is exactly what it's going to be.

PUBLIC EXERCISE IN LOSERDOM (THE FIRST)

We skirt the woods, and head for the sidewalk along the main road. Cars zip past us at forty, forty-five, fifty miles an hour. I wonder if any of the drivers have been drinking too much. I wonder if everyone we see through the wide, clear windshields is going to make it home. My mind floats full of phrases like "massive trauma to the cranium."

Steve Burns apparently lives in Randemwood, the neighborhood directly behind Rallyburger. Once we're in the subdivision, it's easy enough to tell which house is Steve's. There are cars lined up and down the block, two wheels in the street and two on the grass. Music leaks from the house's open windows, and there are people on the front porch talking and laughing. Mostly juniors and seniors.

What are we doing here?

Inside, the party looks pretty much like what you see on TV, which is surprising. People mill around with drinks in their hands, sort of talking. I always thought it was just a Hollywood thing, trying to make high school seem extra cool or something.

Every high school "party" I've ever been to involved pizza and pretzels and canned pop in someone's basement, with their mom and dad upstairs. Maybe some card games. Maybe a movie. Ten to twelve people, tops, who all knew each other already.

There are pretzels here. That's about the only thing that seems familiar. Well, and the guys look mostly the same as usual, dressed in jeans and T-shirts. The girls look fancier than they do at school, in short skirts and slinky tops, or low jeans and tank tops scrunched up to bare their flat stomachs. Lots of jewelry. They're standing around clutching cans of beer or blue plastic cups that almost seem too big for their hands. They move their hips and their arms a little, sort of dancing in place.

"Do you see Cindy?" Alex cranes his neck.

"Be cool, man," I warn him. "I'll keep an eye out."

Steve's house is pretty big. On the first floor alone there's two living rooms, a dining room, a den, a bedroom, and a kitchen. No wonder half of the school fits in here. Steve's parents must be fairly rich, because they go away for the weekend a lot. We've heard tell of Steve Burns's legendary all-night parties. Some people stay until after midnight, it's rumored.

In the kitchen we find a bunch of guys who look like they play on the football team. Patrick is in there. He looks a bit surprised to see me, but he catches my eye and nods. Other than that, we pretty much pretend we've never spoken before.

"Get you something to drink?" Patrick asks. He sweeps his hand over the offerings like a bartender. The kitchen island is littered with bottles of liquor. I read the labels. Vodka. Tequila. Rum. There's also orange juice. Cranberry. Club soda.

Front and center there's a padlocked wooden box with a slot in the top. Alex sticks a couple of bucks in the slot. "Beer," he says. He seems smooth, like he's done it a thousand times. I'm impressed.

Patrick opens a cooler chest on the floor and tosses us two icy cans of Budweiser.

"None for me, thanks." I hand it back.

Patrick shrugs and cracks it open himself. Alex cracks his, too, but doesn't sip. As we leave the kitchen, he still doesn't drink any. I guess it's worth the two bucks to him to hold it and look like he's drinking.

"Do you see her?" he repeats.

"Dude. I'm looking." I get the feeling that this quest for Cindy is somehow going to land us both in some kind of major trouble. The beery smell of this party alone, if it sticks to me, will be good enough for a grounding.

"Let's go to the backyard," Alex says. "Maybe she's out there."

We walk through the dining room to get to the sliding glass doors to the back porch, which is epically huge and full of couples talking and kissing and holding hands and leaning into each other.

"Ew," Alex says. "Let's not."

We turn around, and there she is. Cindy Duncan, in all her supposed glory. I gotta be honest. I don't see it. She has slightly bucked teeth and a pointy nose and her eyes are really close together. She's pretty-ish, but the way Alex goes on about her you'd think she was a runway model. She's wearing a short, strappy dress and carrying a blue cup and smiling. She has good legs, though. That's for sure.

"Hi, Alex."

"Oh. Uh. Hi, uh, Cindy."

"Hi, Cindy," I say.

"Hi, Kermit," she says, still looking at Alex. Then she falters. Looks at me. "Oh gosh. Hi. I'm so sorry about Sheila."

"Thanks." My gaze falls to the carpet. No one has said her name to me in days.

"How are you?" she says. I'm about to tell her "Fine, I guess." But she isn't talking to me anymore.

"I'm good," Alex says. "Great party, eh?"

"Yeah." Cindy twirls one of her dusty brown locks around her finger. Flirty. I take that as a good sign.

I edge away. "I think I'll, um, I'll go get something to drink."

"Okay," Alex says.

"Anyone need anything?"

Cindy shakes her head. "We're good," Alex says. He can't get rid of me fast enough.

Since I'm not actually getting a drink, I don't really have anywhere to go, so I watch from the dining room doorway. Cindy twirls her hair and giggles. She sways back and forth, from one foot to the other. Maybe she's a little drunk already, but it's hard to tell because girls also just kind of do that some- times. Alex is nervous, but he's doing good. Cindy's laughing. Alex gets brave and puts his hand on her arm. You go, buddy. Cindy steps a little closer to him. Yes. Alex leans in and kisses her. I should avert my eyes, but I don't. It's long awaited and lovely. Alex slides his arm around her and with his other hand opens the screen door, steering Cindy out onto the couples' porch.

Part of me cheers, and part of me aches. Not the Sheila part. A new part.

I think it's the part of me that hangs with Alex at Rallyburger every Friday, wondering if now that, too, might be over.

BARTENDER'S CHOICE

"I can get you something soft," Patrick says. He's alone in the large kitchen, with me lingering awkwardly in the doorway.

"Um," I manage to say.

"First time at Steve's?"

"Yeah."

Patrick crosses the room and presses a Solo cup into my hand.

"I can't."

"It's water," he assures me. "You should hydrate."

"I look dehydrated?"

Patrick smiles. "I will give you all my pennies next game if you can tell me the last time you drank a glass of water."

"Um."

He laughs. "Safest bet I ever made."

I sip. "How'd you end up bartender?"

Patrick tugs a dish towel out of the refrigerator door handle. "It's not official. Steve doesn't care if people get their own drinks. But between you and me, I don't really know how to do the party thing." He wipes down the counter. "I like having something to do."

That's a surprise. "You seem like you know everybody."

"This way I get to talk to everyone, but not for that long." He tips up one shoulder. "It's a living." He grins.

I smile back, and it doesn't feel as forced now. Patrick's nice enough. And he *knows*, which means something. The club thing makes sense, here and now.

Growing more comfortable, I ask, "Do you—"

"*O'Hall!*" bellows a voice from the space behind me. A rush of bodies brushes past my shoulder. A fresh wave of popular kids surrounds me, slapping greetings with Patrick and rummaging through the alcohol on display. The kitchen goes from refuge to rumpus.

The beer smell combined with the aura of testosterone starts to get to me. I fade backward, through the doorway into the dining room, chased by a rousing chorus of "Chug! Chug! Chug!"

SLOW-MOTION HORROR SHOW (FOR YOUR EYES ONLY)

Here's what is terrible. Being stranded alone at a drinking party not drinking, while your best friend is hooking up with his crush out on the couples' porch, and your own crush is a guy but no one can know that, and everyone around you is getting progressively drunker but your sister got killed by a drunk driver, so all you can do is stand there alone and witness the drunkenness, hoping none of these drunk people decide they are going to drive home.

It's enough to lead a guy to drink.

Except you can't because you're Baptist, not to mention the thing with your sister that just happened, and you're Baptist, which also makes the whole crush-on-a-guy thing seriously problematic and all of these things add up to no one wanting to talk to you, because it's awkward to talk to the sober guy whose sister just died, so you end up standing alone by a window, constantly resisting the urge to tear down the curtains and start beating people with the rod. So you smile.

Only ninety-five minutes to curfew.

Alex is your best friend. He doesn't mean to be a jackass.

Just breathe.

Then a soft voice in your ear says, "I wasn't sure you'd come."

SWING AND A ... MISS

Tiny heart attacks. Matt Rincorn stands close to me, his arm braced on the window frame behind me. His eyes are bright. "You look like you're about to jump out of your skin," he says.

"No. It's okay."

"I was going to get some air. Wanna come?"

"Outside?" I imagine us on the couples' porch. Matt will throw his arm around me, like Alex did with Cindy. I'll lean against him and look him in the eyes. We'll kiss and I won't care who's looking.

"That's where they keep the air," he says. "Come on."

I shake my head like it's an Etch A Sketch, as if to clear the fantasy from my mind. Kermit: zero. Impure thoughts: one hundred.

My heart pounds, following Matt. To my relief— disappointment?—the "outside" he meant was the front porch, where everything is friendly and wide open and about as uncouple-y as it gets.

By some fluke of fortune, the wooden porch swing is vacant. "Sweet," Matt says. "I dig this thing."

We sit side by side.

"You okay?" Matt says.

"Yeah."

"If you're okay, say 'I'm okay.'" With his toe he starts the porch swing rocking.

I dry my sticky palms on my jeans, without speaking.

"That's what I thought," he says.

"It's been a weird day," I say.

"One day at a time is bullshit," Matt says. "It's one minute at a time. You okay?"

"This minute?" Sitting next to you, outside in the fresh air, beyond the beer smell and the deafening music, with the porch swing creaking and swaying beneath us?

"Yep." Matt smiles.

"I'm okay."

"There you go." Matt lays his arm across the back of the swing, stretching behind me. I glance at it, still amazed at his proximity. It's strange, to have this particular dream come true, right smack in the middle of the nightmare that the rest of my life has become. I glance at his arm again.

"Don't worry. I'm not hitting on you." Matt sways closer to me. The sweet scent of his breath makes me realize he's been drinking. Possibly a lot.

"No, I know."

"Anyway, everyone here is cool with it," he whispers. "We could start making out and no one would give a fuck."

My whole body freezes. Stiff as a board. "I—I—"

Matt laughs. "Relax. I'm kidding. Geez, you are wound tight."

"Sorry." I jerk my bent arms up and down like a robot. "I'm still in factory mode."

He laughs again. "You're funny."

Me?

"I swear I don't usually make kissing jokes," he says. "I don't know what the hell I'm talking about. You seem cool, I guess. Most guys would deck me for saying that."

He keeps calling me cool. I don't know where he's looking, to see that. "It's okay."

"Thanks for not decking me."

"I wouldn't even know what to do with my fists," I say.

Matt laughs harder. "You probably don't get the joke you just made, but it was really awesome."

It was an accidental joke. I mean, I do get it, but I don't know how to admit that to him. I smile. "All I meant is I'm a lover, not a fighter."

Matt sinks into the corner of the rocker, lost in hilarity. "You're killing me, man."

I gaze into the neighborhood twilight, grinning to myself. I can't believe I actually said that. The things that come into my mind can't usually be spoken. For me, this is bold. For me, this is reckless. I'm loving it.

"It's not fair," Matt says, slowly calming himself. "I can't ever say anything about that kind of stuff. Sex stuff. People get all weirded out."

This, I understand. When it's all a big secret, there's nobody to ask about anything. Nobody to talk to, or joke with. "Sorry," I tell him. Sorry for him, and for me.

"It's not like I have a crush on every guy I meet. But I can't even comment if I see a nice ass go by. All my friends get to sit around all day talking about some girl's body. Half an hour it might go on. So-and-so has a great rack. Did you see so-and-so's ass in those jeans? Sometimes I just want to admire an ass, too, okay?"

"So who has a nice ass?" I ask.

"Richie Corner," Matt says automatically. Um, yeah. He totally does. Matt laughs. "But never tell him I said so."

"I won't."

"He would deck me."

"Probably."

"Definitely," Matt says, with an edge to it.

A giggling group of girls spills out from the house. They are tipsy at minimum. One of them is Cindy's friend Crystal, which lets me know Alex is probably having a great time with a nice, soft Cindy right now. Matt and I fall quiet as they tumble past us into the yard.

It's nice on the porch swing. We don't have to really look at each other. But we're together.

As a clump, the girls sit-slash-plop-slash-fall onto the grass. They laugh and chatter about whatever it is girls laugh and chatter about when they're drunk and piled on top of one another on a lawn.

They're far enough away that their voices become sounds mixed into the music and the chatter from the house windows and the people gathered at the other end of the porch.

It's easy enough to simply be. But I don't want us to stop talking.

"It's nice to have a normal conversation," I say.

Matt frowns. "You call this normal? Dude, you are way further gone than I thought."

I blush. Not normal. It's special.

"I just meant thanks for talking to me. This isn't really my kind of scene."

Matt laughs. "News flash. I'm surprised you even came."

"My friend Alex wanted to."

"Yeah. Where is he anyway?"

"Sticking his tongue down Cindy Duncan's throat." It comes out more resentful than I mean it to. "Whatever. It's not like I want to be at home anyway."

"Word." Matt sticks out his fist and I pound it. "I admit, I was hoping you'd show. I'm in Spanish with Alex. I told him you guys should come on by, but I didn't think you would."

"You invited us?"

He sways toward me, shifting the motion of the swing. "What if I did?"

"Then I'll know who to blame for my current predicament." I can't let myself believe in the other possibility—he wanted to see me.

Matt's face is strangely close to mine, for one suspended moment. Then he laughs, flopping backward.

"Fuck. Just ignore me. I'm wasted." He closes his eyes. His body relaxes into the opposite corner, arm still stretched behind me.

"You okay?"

"Hmm? Yeah. Great." He stirs. "I took a couple shots before. Before I came to talk to you."

"Oh."

"They're just catching up," he says. "I'm good now. It's good."

"How'd you get here?" I ask.

"What?" he says.

"Do you need a ride home?"

"Oh." He points at an angle across the street. "No. That's my house."

It's a big house. As big as Steve's, maybe. Brown bricks on the front. Tan siding. Roof tiles in a sort of maroon or something. Hard to tell in the darkness.

"So, you come here often?" I ask, trying to keep my voice from sounding overly husky.

"Yeah, man. Steve's parties are my jam." Matt taps my neck with his fingers and my whole body reacts. "This is the best one yet, though."

NON-TOXIC MASCULINITY

Matt rocks us gently, his fingertips teasing the collar of my shirt as we talk into the near darkness. He's pretty drunk, I think, and I'm not even sure he's aware of the way he's touching me. I hold myself as still as possible, not wanting to break the spell.

Alex breaks it for me. Suddenly there he is, standing over us. "It's time," he says.

"Time?" I echo.

Alex holds up his wrist toward me as if he's wearing a watch, dragging Cindy's hand along for the exercise. He has his other arm around her waist and she's leaning against his shoulder. Her hair is mussed, her lipstick smudged, and she's smiling.

"Looks like someone had some fun," Matt says. He squeezes my shoulder, then lets his hand drop away.

"We have a curfew," I say. "Not sure how everyone else gets away with staying so late." It's not yet eleven, but we have to walk back to Rallyburger before my mom arrives and wonders where we went.

"The key is to have parents who don't give a shit," Matt says. "It's a beautiful thing."

It's hard to tell if he's serious or not.

"How's Cindy getting home?" I ask, standing up. She turns her face into Alex's chest and sighs.

"They have a DD," Alex assures me, naming a junior girl I know from church.

"You guys have a good night." Matt waves.

I fight the impulse to lean down and kiss him goodbye, like Alex is now doing with Cindy. I'm not even sure he'd mind. But we can't all have nice things, can we?

Soften up, baby bro, Sheila's voice says. *Live a little.*

Shut up, I tell her. There are so many things she will never know or understand.

Alex delivers Cindy to the group of giggling girls on the lawn. They fold her right into the pile and within seconds, it's as if we guys never existed.

We walk past the line of cars again. This time, there are people making out in some of them. "Whoa, check it out," Alex says. "We could totally prank them."

"Open the door so they'd fall out?"

He laughs. "Yeah. If we never want to be invited anywhere cool again." Then his laugh kind of fades. "Anyway, I'd never really do that to anyone, especially now that I know what it's like . . ." He looks away.

"So what happened with Cindy?"

"Nothing really. We made out."

I slug his shoulder. "That doesn't sound like nothing."

Alex's grin rivals the crescent moon. "Okay, it was great."

"That was your dream, dude. Now you've kissed and it's like it was nothing?"

Alex goes quiet. "It's just—this kinda messed-up thing happened."

No need to ask what. Now that he's brought it up it's only a matter of time before it all comes out of him. I wait through the silence.

"She was already kinda tipsy, but when she finished the drink she had I went and got us another round. She asked me to," he adds quickly.

"Okay."

"I got a second beer and I got her some of that punch stuff she was having."

"Um-hmm." I pretend not to be surprised about Alex actually drinking. While he was having beer, I was walking a goddamn plank of impure thoughts, so who am I to get all holier than thou?

"And the guy who mixed it up for me goes, when he's handing Cindy's drink to me, he goes, 'It's pretty strong, just so you know.' So I go, 'Okay.' And there were a bunch of other guys in the kitchen and they start cheering. One of them leans over and sniffs the cup and goes, 'Hell yeah! One more of those and she'll do anything you want. Go plant your flag.'" Alex looks at the ground. "And I didn't know what to say."

"Ew," I say. "'Go plant your flag'?"

"That's messed up, right?"

"Um, yeah."

"I mean, I wasn't trying to, you know, make it with Cindy. I really like her and wanted to see her and stuff. That's all."

"Yeah."

"So, when I gave her the cup back I told her it was mixed strong, and she was like, 'Cool, thanks.'"

"And she took it?"

"Yeah. She was, like, happy about it."

"So?"

Alex stares into the darkness. "So, it's embarrassing."

"You can tell me."

"It just got up in my head. All that shit Sheila is always—" He breaks off. "Sorry, I mean was." Another moment of silence. "Sorry, it's just that she was always going on about how men take advantage, you know, and how there's fucked-up cultural expectations . . ."

"Her toxic masculinity tirade?"

"Yeah." Alex laughs. "Did she hate all men?"

The smile sneaks up on me. "I don't think all men, just the way some guys are."

"Hate the sin, love the sinner, and all?"

That strikes a chord in me, deep. "Something like that."

"Anyway." Alex sighs. "It was like, all of that. Exactly that. Cindy was drunk and seemed fine with anything. It would have been really easy, probably, to just . . ."

"Yeah."

"But . . . it was kinda messed up."

"Yeah."

"And so I totally mind-fucked myself out of, you know . . ."

"Says who?"

Alex shrugs. "I mean, she kinda wanted to do something more, I think. But we were in the yard and there were people around. It was weird."

"How so?"

"She kept grabbing at my fly, but she was pretty drunk."

"What did you do?"

"I mean, I kind of let her, but I also couldn't tell, like, if she really wanted to, or if she was just too messed up to realize what she was doing and stop." He rubs his forehead. "We ended up out by the shed, in the grass. Way out back, mostly alone, but not totally."

"And you were . . . ?"

"Kissing. Touching. I got to see her bra and touch . . ." He pauses. "But then I kind of blew it."

"She wanted to stop?"

"No. We stopped kissing for a minute while I was, you know, dealing with the sight of her boobs and everything—"

"Sounds great."

"It was fucking great. And then she started laughing and said the sky was spinning. So I said, 'Hey, let's sit up for a minute,' but then she had a hard time getting up. So I pulled her dress back on and we just lay in the grass and looked at the clouds for a while."

He runs his hand through his hair and shrugs. "Don't tell anybody."

"What, that you're too good a guy to take advantage of a drunk girl?" I roll my eyes. "Yeah, we better not let that horror story leak out."

"Come on, you know what I mean."

"Yeah, but, like . . . it's kinda shitty, right? All that stupid pressure."

"Yeah," he agrees. "I thought maybe we'd do it in the back

seat sometime, after I get my license. Or in the park or some-thing. After a real date. Just her and me, and . . . I don't know. Not like a coincidence, right? Like we made a plan and we wanted to? I'd get some flowers and shit. Whatever she wants."

"Aww," I say. "You're a romantic."

"Shut up," Alex says.

"All bullshit aside?" I tell him. "That date plan sounds like a fucking great night. Way better than a random hand job with a bunch of people watching. I bet Cindy will think so, too."

"Or maybe I blew it," Alex moans. "And I'll never get the chance."

"Nah," I say. "It's better to regret doing the right thing than doing the wrong thing."

"I guess."

"You guess?"

"No, yeah. I know you're right."

I slug him in the arm. "Call her in the morning. Say you want to take her out. She'll love it."

CHAUFFEUR DUTY

Alex and I are sitting on the bench outside Rallyburger by the time Mom pulls up. Alex swiped a breath mint from the bowl by the cash register in the thirty seconds before they locked the door. Technically they close at eleven thirty, but they stop seating new parties after eleven.

I ride in the front and Alex in the back. All the more distance between his beer breath and Mom's nose.

"Thanks, Mrs. Sanders," he says, hopping out at his house.

"Good night, Alex."

When we're alone, Mom says, "Did you have fun?"

"Yeah," I say, a little surprised to find it's true. Matt saved my night.

"Good. I'm glad you're seeing your friends."

This is when I normally would dish to Mom that Alex has a girlfriend. I'd swear her to secrecy and then stubbornly decline to provide any further details, despite her clamoring. We'd both arrive home grinning.

Instead, we're quiet.

A gray car speeds through a yellow light across the intersection in front of us. Mom's hands go tight on the wheel. Could leave it at that, but I'm on edge and maybe feeling a little confrontational.

"You should let me get rides," I say. "You hate chauffeur duty." Now more than ever.

"It's fine." She flexes her fingers and looks both ways a few more times before proceeding.

"No. I need to live my own life," I say. "So get used to it."

THEN: MIDNIGHT LESSONS (ONE MONTH AGO)

In the night I curl up with my laptop and headphones, dim the screen, and pull up the blankets. The internet is my dark, secret boyfriend.

I watch and rewatch the episode of *A Million Little Things* where Danny comes out. Then fast-forward through *Schitt's Creek* season four, slowing to catch all the sweet moments between David and Patrick. Then a few episodes of *Sex Education*, which makes my pulse tick upward. To be out, to be open, is portrayed as a thing of beauty in these spaces, and it's almost possible to believe. But in the real world it's still a problem, still a mystery.

I'll have to sleep at some point, because people need to sleep, but my mind needs this knowledge more than rest. There's an old show, *Queer as Folk*, with a lot of club scenes and sex scenes and nakedness. It's the closest I can bring myself to watching . . . well, anyway, I turn the sound extra low and let it stir me.

NOW: UNDER COVERS

Friday night, after Rallyburger, used to be my time. Alone, tucked in bed, with the whole world open to my imagination. A fountain of possibilities at my fingertips, a mere click away.

Now I can't focus on any of it. My head feels too full and my heart too heavy to take in any fictional drama.

It's hard to imagine what fires might have been fueled, in the before time, to be touched by a boy the way Matt touched me tonight. But even that feels distant now, like a dream. Like a fiction itself. Unreal.

The laptop rests cold beside me.

I close my eyes and sleep.

DORKOPTERIX

In the dream, I burst into Sheila's bedroom, ranting at her about something exciting. I feel the excitement, but I don't know what it's about. But it annoys her immediately.

"Shut up, dorkopterix."

"Dork-a-what?"

"Dorkopterix. You're a total dorkopterix."

"What is that, like a dorky dinosaur?"

"It's you, dorkopterix."

"That's not a thing. You just made it up."

"Maybe I like how it sounds, dorkopterix."

"Maybe I should punch you in the face."

"Go ahead and try, dorkopterix. You'd have to stand on a table."

"I can jump pretty high."

"Dorkopterix is a land-bound reptile. No jumping ability."

"I can too jump."

"No can do, dorkopterix."

"There's no such thing as a dorky dinosaur. Dinosaurs are awesome."

"They were until you came along, dorkopterix."

"Stop calling me that."

"Dorkopterix."

"Stupid-head."

"Oh, that's original."

"Stupidopterix."

"There's no such thing as a stupid dinosaur, you dorkopterix."

"Mom!"

"Only dorkopterixes tattle. Tattle-o-saurus."

"If there's a tattle-o-saurus, then they're the ones who tattle. Not dorkopterix."

"Fair enough."

"Ha."

"So you are accepting your place in the reptile kingdom as dorkopterix?"

"Yes, and dorkopterix is the ruler of all the land."

"Dinosaur land?"

"Yes."

"That's tyrannosaurus."

"T. rex is the king of lizards. I am the prime minister."

"What are you talking about?"

"In England they have a king and a prime minister. The king is big and showy, like T. rex, but the prime minister is actually in charge."

"How do you know that?"

"I know things."

"I can't believe you know that. You're such a dorkopterix."

"So what are you going to be?"

"What?"

"What kind of dinosaur? You don't have to be stupidopterix anymore."

"I'm not a dinosaur, you dweeb."

"Please. Call me dorkopterix. Aren't we going to play?"

"Play?"

"Dinosaurs."

"God, no. I have a *life*."

"You started it."

"No I didn't."

"Yes you did."

"No."

"Yes."

"No."

"Yes."

"Arrgh. I said 'shut up, dorkopterix—'"

"See."

"—because I was hoping you'd shut up and leave me alone."

"Didn't work, did it?"

"Oh my God. *Get out of my room.*"

"Ha ha ha."

"*Dorkopterix* is such a perfect word for what you are."

"Ha ha ha."

"Would you please go?"

"Ha ha ha."

"Mom!"

"Tattle-o-saurus alert! Tattle-o-saurus alert!"

"You little—"

"Dorkopterix?"

"Oh my God."

"Zzzzzzzz. Boring-o-saurus. That's you."

SANDERS, PARTY OF THREE

It's not weird that Sheila's place at the dinner table is empty. It's been empty since the middle of July when she left for her pre-college band geek summer camp.

I mean, I've already spent the better part of three months eating dinner across from Ghost Sheila, and gotten to the point where I could deal with it, no problem. So dinnertime is one of the times that feel normal.

But sometimes, on Saturdays, we go out for dinner. So we're sitting with our buzzer in the steakhouse lobby, grazing on peanuts and vaguely watching the Notre Dame game. No one says it, but it's our first dinner out since Sheila died. That's not really significant, except that every first is significant.

"What is everyone looking forward to this coming week?" Mom says, in a bald attempt to sound normal. Dad and I stare up at the screen.

"It's not their day," Dad says, after the Irish fail to convert fourth and inches at the fifteen-yard line.

"Weird they didn't take the field goal," I agree. "They can't put a scoring drive together today to save their lives." It's just an expression, of course, but my head buzzes afterward all the same. To save a life. To escape death. So many things we used to say without thinking land differently now.

Mom sighs and tosses a handful of peanut shells to the floor, too hard.

"What, honey?" Dad flicks his gaze away from the screen.

Mom smiles, tight. The buzzer goes off and we walk to the hostess stand.

A light-brown-skinned, college-aged girl smiles and greets us. "Sanders, party of three?"

Dad bursts into tears.

THEN: CRAB WEEK (SEVEN YEARS AGO)

"Fish is gross," I complain, kicking at the back of the driver's seat. "Why can't we go to the steakhouse?"

"It's Sheila's turn to pick the restaurant," Mom says, putting up with my minor assault. "You picked last week."

"Crab week, baby!" Sheila sings. It's crab week at Red Lobster, and my sister is all about crab these days. It's weird. She used to be like me and protest all seafood. She also used to let me into her room anytime, and now she keeps the door closed and yells at me to go away a lot. I don't know what happens to a person when they turn twelve, but I don't like it.

"They have chicken fingers," Mom reminds me.

Ordering chicken fingers at Red Lobster is about as smart as ordering seafood from a hot dog cart.

"Ew."

"You love chicken fingers," Dad says.

"Not all chicken fingers are created equal," I inform him.

"You should try the crab," Sheila says. "It's sooooo delicious."

"Ew to the hundredth power." I knock her elbow off the armrest between us. She shoves mine back, trying to take over. As usual, she wins.

Hmph. "I know! I'll have the chocolate chip cookie and ice cream for dinner." At least their desserts are good.

"Not likely, sir." Mom glances at me in the rearview.

"Fine. I'll have the shrimp," I grumble, crossing my arms and shrinking against the car door.

"Looks like crab week has begun," Dad quips from the front passenger seat.

Everybody laughs. Even me.

NOW: A SIDE OF FRUIT

A short, stocky blond guy with canyon-sized dimples pops up beside our table. "Hey, y'all. I'm Adam, and I'll be your server tonight."

My gut clenches. He's impossibly cute. Farm-fresh looks with slightly incongruous effeminate mannerisms.

"Y'all know what you want to drink?"

We order a round of Sprites. Adam holds the menu pad in one hand and flaps his pen hand at us as he talks us through the nightly specials. Dad's watching Adam, and I'm watching Dad. Adam's soft wrist circles wave delicately through the air in my peripheral vision. Dad's gaze smacks of disapproval.

"I'll give y'all a minute to decide on dinner," Adam says. Then he sweeps away, hips rocking like a runway model's.

"Dinner, with a side of fruit," Dad murmurs, with a hint of a smirk.

I smile, because I'm supposed to.

"Hush," Mom says. "He seems like a perfectly nice young man."

"I didn't say he wasn't. I'm sure he's 'perfectly nice.'" Dad mimics her, letting his wrist flop downward as he speaks.

And with that I'm spiraling, down down down into the sea of my own poisoned heart.

BORROWED TIME

Sunday I'm still in bed at noon with the covers pulled tight to my chin. Mom knocked when it was time to wake up and again when it was time to leave for church, but it's not hard right now to ignore that.

I'm living on borrowed time, that much I know for sure. The hammer will drop eventually. But the relief at having these mornings free and alone can't be quantified. I don't need to be in a big white building, staring at a cross, to think about life and death and sin and suffering. Those thoughts are with me all the time, and all I want is to escape them, not to lean in and fucking sing about it.

As it is, I lie quietly in my sinful bed, thinking my sinful thoughts, touching my sinful body, and letting my imagination carry me, since I know I won't be interrupted.

BAT SIGNAL

There's nothing written on the ceiling but staring at it must do something for my brain because it's all I'm able to do for a while afterward.

When I get out of the shower, my parents are home. The TV is on, playing NFL football, one of the early games. I'm hungry, but it takes me a few minutes to mentally steel myself to go down there. I'm sure there will be updates about the various elders and an "everybody asked about you" speech from Mom that I'll have to endure, somehow, without losing my shit or talking back.

My phone zings. Text message from Patrick:

-1 EMERGENCY MEETING. JANNA'S HOUSE.

WHEN?

NOW, DOOFUS.

Two seconds later, he adds:

BRING SNACKS.

I jerk on a pair of jeans and tumble down to the kitchen. It occurs to me to wonder what sort of emergency requires stopping to gather snacks, but I do it.

I toss Wheat Thins and string cheese into a paper grocery sack. They look small and lonely down at the bottom of the huge bag, so I crawl into the pantry to my bottom-shelf snack stash and grab some pretzels, a bag of baby oranges, a pack of M&M's, and an open bag of Cheetos that might be stale because I totally forgot they were in here, so I haven't been eating them.

"What are you doing?" Mom asks.

I flinch, feeling like a raccoon caught rifling through the trash bin. "Um, I have to go out." I turn toward her voice, but I don't see her.

Oh. She's lying on the floor between the kitchen island and the stove.

"What are *you* doing?"

"Making a sandwich," she says, like it's totally normal to do that while horizontal. On the island there's the bread, a jar of mayonnaise, and a table knife. The package of turkey slices rests on her stomach. I pick it up, step over her, and finish the sandwich for her.

"Out where?" Mom says. "Since when do you go 'out'?"

"Something came up, with a friend."

"Right now? Kerm, I—" She moves her hand in a way that means, *look at me.* As I do, incongruous images clash in my head. Two hours ago, Mom managed to look perky as hell on the way out the door to church. *See?* I want to tell her. *This is what you get.*

"Well, you look . . . kinda busy," I acknowledge. "It's fine. I have a ride."

"You know the rule." Her eyes are closed.

"Mom—"

My phone rings. Matt. "I'm out front," he says. "Hurry up."

"Um. Can I go?" I say to Mom, setting the sandwich plate on her stomach. "It's kind of important."

She frowns up at me. "It's snowing."

"My friend Matt is picking me up."

"I don't know Matt," Mom says. "Who is Matt?"

"He's a really safe driver," I promise. "And he lives barely a mile away. I can walk to his place if you say I have to. But it's really cold. And snowy, apparently. And there's no sidewalk part of the way."

Mom hates it when I try to walk on the main road, even though people do it all the time and it's perfectly fine. She's convinced some car won't see me and will randomly go off the road at the exact moment I'm passing by. I sneakily do it anyway sometimes. Mom's paranoia is pointless. It didn't save my sister, who was practically perfect in every way Mom wanted her to be. Unlike me.

"Who is Matt?" she repeats.

"He's outside right now," I tell her. "You can go meet him. He's super responsible."

She purses her lips. "Write down the phone number where you'll be."

I wave my cell in her face. "Duh. I have my phone."

"I don't care," she snaps. "This Matt. I want to talk to his mother."

"His mother's dead," I tell her. Mom flinches. "Yeah, we have something in common. So I'm going *out*." I scoop up the sack of snacks and stomp toward the front door. I yank my parka off the coat tree and slam my free arm into one sleeve. Good enough to get out of here.

Matt reaches across and pushes open the door for me. I ease it the rest of the way open with my foot and jump in, pushing the grocery sack between my legs, down into the footwell.

Mom doesn't even pull on a coat. She comes after me, trotting down the front walk, her feet stuffed into an unlaced pair of tennis shoes that might actually have belonged to Sheila.

"God," I mutter. "Drive. Go. Go now."

Instead, Matt flicks the button that rolls down the passenger-side window. "Hi, Mrs. Sanders."

"Matt?" She bends to peer in the window.

"Yes. I'm Matthew Rincorn." He leans across me and stretches a hand out the window. Mom shakes it. Then her fingers flutter to rest on the lip of the window, clinging to the door.

"I—" she says. "I want—" Her voice stalls.

"It's nice to meet you, ma'am," Matt says. "I'll have Kermit back by nine, is that all right?"

"Um, well . . ."

"Earlier, if you like," he says. "We're just having some fun."

Snowflakes dampen her arms, neck, and shoulders. She looks up at the sky. "I'm afraid it's going to get worse."

"It's not far, ma'am," Matt confirms. "We'll be all right. He can call you when we get there."

"I'll text you," I tell her. "I promise."

"Drive safely," Mom says.

"Ma'am, I know I have your son's life in my hands, so to speak," he says. "I take the responsibility very seriously."

"Okay," she says, relaxing her grip. She looks at me. "Well, how about eight? I don't want you out so long after dark."

Eleven's my normal weekend curfew; I intend to protest. But it's Sunday, so it's a school night.

"Sure, but I don't have to be home until ten," Matt says. "When I bring him back early, can the two of us hang out here until then?"

"Yes," Mom says on a sigh of relief. "I'd prefer that. I'll make pizza."

"Sounds great."

"Come here." Mom grabs me and kisses my face. "I love you, sweetie." Gross display of affection. I tolerate it, though mortified. Matt looks away.

Mom rushes back inside. She must be freezing.

"I'm so sorry," I tell him. "My mom's a total freak."

Matt shrugs. "She can't help it. She loves you, like she said." He pulls out of the driveway real slow. Mom waves to us from behind the screen door, and I feel good enough to wave back. It strikes me how smooth Matt just was. I'd have ended up yelling and screaming and probably not allowed to go anywhere ever again.

"That was good," I tell him. "Like, amazingly good." If I could handle Mom that easily, my life would be totally different.

"Yeah, I'm great with women." Matt laughs, bursting and loud. "It's such a fucking waste. Isn't that always the way?"

I laugh, too. "Well, if you have any pointers, I'll take them."

Matt steals a glance at me. A strange, distant expression. Like the transmission console between us is a much wider gulf than it should be. I wonder, in the wake of it, when he returns his eyes to the whitening road, what he's thinking. I wonder if he knows my comment was kind of a forced thing. The thing I figured a normal guy would say.

GOD OF SNACKS

"Geez, Sanders, are you prepping for the apocalypse?" Patrick says. He peers into the enormous sack of groceries I've brought.

"What? You said bring snacks."

"I meant, like, a pack of Oreos or something."

"He's an overachiever," Matt says. "We're lucky he's wasting his time with a bunch of losers like us."

"The Cheetos might be stale," I say by way of self-defense.

"This is an extraordinary feast," Simon declares, taking it upon himself to test the Cheetos. He proclaims them "still good."

Meanwhile, Janna sits on the edge of her bed, trying and failing to choke back tears.

"So much for not talking about it," I say.

"Oh, we're not going to talk about it," Patrick says. "That's the whole point."

And we don't.

Simon scrolls through music on Janna's laptop, tossing new songs onto the playlist that's running in the background. Celia brushes Janna's hair while Matt and Patrick argue about the row of stuffed animals on her bookshelf, trying to guess their names.

Janna's tears are magnetic. I can't stop watching her cry. It's never-ending. Tears are supposed to be this finite thing that comes and goes. How much water can there be in one person's body?

She's not even wiping them away, just letting them fall onto her shirt. Her shoulders shake and she grips the edge of the mattress, all but choking on sadness. It's magnificent.

That kind of release is something I crave, but it feels so far out of reach. I guess Janna's had a couple years of practice.

An echo in the core of me does cry. *Years?*

And suddenly I don't understand. How she looks is how I feel, or how I *would* feel if the terrible things inside of me were allowed to come out, which they're not. But this is fresh grief, and it's been years for Janna.

Years?

Like Matt said the other night, I'm still sitting here trying to get through each fucking moment without a total collapse. But suddenly I see a path rolling out ahead of me, a steep, breath-stealing staircase with no way to turn back and no end in sight.

"Death fucking sucks," I blurt out.

THE FIRST RULE OF GRIEF CLUB

Silence. They all look at me.

"That's the one you get," Janna sobs. She reaches for the speaker remote and slams up the music.

"I don't think you understand how it works," Simon adds. "Never means never."

"Talk to your friends about it," Celia says. "This is where we go to get away from it."

"I don't have a lot of other friends," I admit. "Not like you guys."

Patrick stands up. "Okay, Sanders. You're with me. C'mon." He leads me out of the bedroom, downstairs, and into the kitchen. He opens the fridge and starts pulling out drinks. Juice, soda, sports drink.

"So you're the bartender here, too?"

"See what's in the pantry," he instructs me.

More of everything, not cold.

"What do you want?" Patrick asks.

There's no way to even begin answering that question. "Uh, world peace?"

He grins. "To drink, doofus. What do you want to drink?"

"Oh. The Sprite, I guess."

He hands me the cold two-liter of Sprite, two sports drinks, and the juice carton. Then he goes to the pantry and pulls out replacements of each and pops them into the fridge. He grabs a glass from the cupboard and fills it with water, then does a splayed-spider thing with his other hand in the cupboard and comes up with five other glasses, held by the rims.

"Just be chill in the room," he says as we start walking back. "It's weird, but this is what we do."

"I didn't mean to say anything," I tell him. "Normally I'm really good at, you know, not talking."

He nods, like he gets it. "You're not wrong," he adds. "Death does suck."

"Matt says you guys hang out one-on-one from time to time." Maybe it's weird to say this, but it just comes out of me. That's a thing that's happening today, and I really gotta get a handle on it.

"Oh. Huh."

"What?"

"Yeah, we don't really do that," Patrick says. "We do the group thing mostly. I don't know why he said that."

"Oh."

"The group's not perfect, I know," Patrick says.

It seems pretty perfect to me. "It's great, actually."

"Yeah. What I said is, it's not perfect."

"Meaning?"

"Meaning, it's not a fix for anything. It just helps." Patrick shakes his head. "We still all have to go through it. And that's lonely."

I shrug. "Putting the card in the box, it felt like something was going to come out of it."

"That's the thing," Patrick says. "There is nothing. Just time."

How much time? I want to ask.

"Pretending to be normal is unbearable sometimes, is all."

"Janna's a bit of a mess, clearly, but Matt's doing just fine."

Patrick looks at me. "Matt's not fine," he says. "I know you can't tell yet. Just . . . remember that I said that."

We push back into the bedroom, carrying drinks for all. Matt, Janna, and Patrick drink the sports drink. Celia chugs half the glass of water, then pours some juice into it. Simon takes juice and tops it off with some of my Sprite.

The thing I like best about this moment is that Patrick clearly knew without asking what everyone would have, and exactly how it would go. We graze on my snacks and I feel like a part of something.

Janna goes to the closet and pulls out the red-and-green box of Apples to Apples. She holds it up and shrugs.

"That'll do," Simon says. "If it's what you want."

She nods and hands him the box. I've heard of it but never played before. It's a silly game of matching words with emotions, which is pretty freaking ironic for a group that never wants to talk about anything.

So we play the silly game and Janna just cries through it and we all pretend there's nothing wrong. Because what else can you do but just keep living forward?

AFTERMATH

"**What the hell** was that?" I ask.

"An emergency," Matt says in the car on the way home.

"She was crying when we got there and crying when we left. We didn't actually do anything to help."

"It helped. Sometimes you feel like crap and you just don't want to be alone."

"I don't think I'd want five people hanging around watching me cry like that."

"It's not always like that. That's just Janna. She's a crier."

I'm supposed to be able to cry, I think. It's normal to cry when someone dies.

Snow falls in sheets outside the window. The car heater's blowing and the radio's blurring softly, and Matt has his hands tight on the wheel, peering between the wiper blades at the disappearing road.

"Since we don't talk about it, I guess we'll never know what it was about."

"Sometimes you just want someone there with you, like I said. But it's not too hard to do the math on this one."

He waves his hand at the windshield. Out the window, the swirling snow flurries. It's not really too bad, if a bit heavy for the season's first snowfall. Just a few days ago we were sitting out on the porch, enjoying a crisp autumn evening.

"When it snows it's hard for her," Matt says. "Like how you feel about drinking."

"What?" I say.

Matt looks at me funny. "You get all tense and freaked out around booze. You didn't know?"

"Because I don't drink?"

"You act like it's a religious thing, but you're not that religious. It's about your sister."

For a moment it's just the snowfall, the heater, the blur of the radio. Him calling me "not that religious" strikes an uncomfortable chord. How can he see that? As far as the world is concerned, Kermit Sanders is the poster child for Christian teenhood. My face is literally on one of the testimonial recruitment ads that our church runs in the school paper. There's a blown-up copy of it in the church lobby, too.

"So, you think she'll be all right? Janna."

"Sure. Like I said, she's just a crier."

"I never cried," I admit.

"People deal with things differently. Patrick likes to hit things. Celia makes weird art. Simon's a computer geek; I don't know what the hell he does."

"Ha."

"Trust me. Someday you'll have an emergency. And we'll come."

"Do you have emergencies?"

"Naw." Matt grins. "I'm invincible."

PIZZA

We're home before seven. Mom is pleased we're early, though
she tries to act chill. Tragically, Mom does not really do chill.
She has two pizzas in the fridge, all set up and ready to bake.

"I made one the way Kermit likes it—Hawaiian with extra
cheese—but the other is plain. We can put anything you like on
it, Matt." She starts listing off topping options I wouldn't have
expected us to have on hand. Did she go shopping? That would
be weird.

Even when we go sit in the living room with Dad to catch
up on football, she can't stop fussing over us. Bringing drinks.
Chips and salsa. A cheese plate. She's kicked into some kind of
manic hostess gear I've never seen before.

"Mom, relax. We're fine."

"Everything is great, Mrs. Sanders," Matt confirms.

At the table, Matt sits in Sheila's seat, because that's the
fourth chair at the table. Having that space filled is weirder than
not at this point.

"Let us pray," Dad says, laying both hands palm up on the
tabletop. Mom follows suit.

Oh God. This never occurred to me. A whole beat passes

before my fingers do what is expected, reaching out to grasp theirs.

Matt meets my gaze across the table as he takes my parents' hands. Oh God. Is it possible to stare an apology?

My ears burn red as my mouth moves automatically over the pre-meal song we sing. A blessing, sung by my dad's family before every meal for as long as anyone knows.

One corner of Matt's mouth twitches up, but otherwise his expression is static, his attention fixed on me. Great, now he knows what my singing voice sounds like. That's bound to be a deal-breaker.

What deal? Sheila says. *There is no deal, you little chicken.*

My parents bow their heads as the song ends and Dad finishes the prayer with a few spoken words, but we are unmoving, Matt and I. Our gazes entwine across the table as firmly as clasped hands in their own right. The words of prayer swirl heavy around the pizza platter and the place settings, but the two of us rise above. The usual feeling I get when we pray—that horrible, drowning feeling—never comes. I'm lifted out of it.

CAROUSEL

Matt Rincorn is sitting on my bed. My *bed*. Where just this morning I lay under the covers, thinking about him and—

"I was gonna suggest laser tag for today, but that plan went off the rails," Matt says, picking a piece of lint off my bedspread. "How about after school tomorrow?"

"Great." I'm trying to focus on the hot guy in the room but at the same time it's impossible not to glance around. What does my room look like to a person who's never seen it before? Is there anything embarrassing that's too familiar for me to notice?

My room is messy but not too bad, really. Sheila's is always messier. Was.

"Kermit Sanders's inner sanctum," Matt muses. "Places I never thought I'd be."

It's too intense, him saying that. As if he's thought of me. As if he's wondered.

"This is me," I answer, pushing past the discomfort of wondering how he feels about what he sees.

He touches each color on my Tae Kwon Do belt rack. White, yellow, green. My blue is tied to the waist of my uniform, currently hanging from the closet doorknob.

"Thought you were a lover, not a fighter," he says.

"Tae Kwon Do teaches you to fight but the ethos of the discipline promotes peace."

"Oooh," he says, not quite mockingly, but with a hint of tone. "You're such a good guy, aren't you?"

"What does that mean?"

Matt shrugs. "Nothing bad. You seem really earnest about everything. That's all." He moves toward my bookcase and runs his finger over the spines on the top shelf. Above it hangs my collection of framed scripture quotes. About a dozen, in different sizes, shapes, and styles or fonts. Matt stands still for a time, appearing to read them. "I mean, look at this wall. Next you're gonna tell me you've got Jesus on speed dial."

"Maybe I did, once." I shift in place. Is he looking too closely, or not closely enough?

"Hey, this is neat." Matt crosses to the dresser and spins my LEGO carousel. It was a Christmas gift from Sheila a couple years ago. Still one of my all-time favorites.

"Thanks."

"Did you ever ride the carousel at the Children's Museum?" he asks.

"Yeah, a few times." Floating fragments of impressions strike me. The memory of standing in line for what felt like ages, and then racing to get one of the mechanized horses that goes up and down. Waving at Mom and Dad over and over, each time we passed where they stood.

"I used to like it there," Matt says, stroking the horses' tiny manes.

Round and round, up and down. It's close to how I feel right now. Having him here, amid the swirl of everything.

"We could go there, if you wanted." Indy's not that far away. We could get there and back in an afternoon.

"Yeah," Matt says absently. Perhaps he's already there in his mind, like I am.

THEN: PUTTING IT UP
(FOUR YEARS AGO)

"A little to the left," Sheila says. "If you want it centered."

She sits on my bed monitoring my progress. We measured, we marked, we nailed, and now: the moment of truth.

I nudge the last frame over, to center it. It's my favorite, from I Timothy 4:12. *Let no one look down on you because you are young, but set an example for the believers in your speech, conduct, love, purity, and faith.*

"What do you think?"

"Doesn't matter what I think," Sheila says. "It's your room."

I climb off the stepladder and back away to take it all in. I spent hours choosing the quotes, designing and printing each page, and then picking out and sizing the matching frames from a series online.

"It's awesome."

"There you go," she says. "We did good."

"But what do you think?"

Sheila smiles. "Oh, I don't know. That's a whole lot of Jesus, Kerm. You sure?"

I was sure.

NOW: TEARING IT DOWN

Matt leaves and an itch starts under my skin. Can't stop it. Can't shake it.

Him being here made me see everything anew. And I can't stop looking.

I've seen myself through his eyes now and while it thrilled me to the core, it also showed me that I've become out of touch with certain things in my landscape. My wall of scripture quotes has been up forever, so much so that they faded into the background.

The light from my bedside lamp casts a glow off the corners of each frame. What they meant to me still echoes and yet that glow has become a glare—too hot to handle.

I roll out of bed, letting my hands do what my heart can't.

Glass rattles and shatters in the frames as I throw them to the floor, one on top of the other.

O WISE ONE

In the dream, Sheila's sitting on a pillar, like a first-century ascetic monk. It's not a tall pillar; standing at the base of it, I'm on eye level with her toes. Her legs cross in lotus position, hands resting palm-up on her knees. It is supposed to make her seem wise.

"Speak to me, O Wise One." How annoying, to have to refer to her as such.

She grins. Her eyes drift closed. She falls as still as her corpse was when I had to go and look at it in the funeral home. In the dream, she still looks like herself, though. Not painted fake and frozen. Not the freaky Sheila death mask that springs from the back of my mind like a jack-in-the-box at the most inopportune moments.

"I'd like for you to calm down," she says. "It's all going to work out eventually."

"Yeah, right."

"Yeah. Right."

"You don't have any proof of that."

"I have proof of everything now."

"Yeah?"

She opens her eyes. "No, doofus. You think I'm all-seeing just because I'm dead? I'm totally bullshitting you."

"That's mean."

"Don't you think you'll be happier if you just tell them?"

"Either happier or more miserable, depending on how it goes."

"They love you."

"They hate gays."

"They don't hate gays. They believe what the church tells them."

"Which is to hate gays."

"Well . . . yeah."

"Soooo, how am I supposed to . . . ?"

"Buy Dad a book about it."

"Do you think that will help?"

"Worth a try."

"*Try* means there's a possibility of failing."

"Do your homework. Prep for class. You're an honor student, aren't you?"

"That doesn't help me."

"I'm not here to help you."

"I thought . . ."

"Dude, I'm dead. I'm just here to annoy you."

"Sheil."

"Kerm."

"Just tell me what to do."

"Tell yourself."

"Please."

"Tell Mom and Dad."

"I can't."

"Well, what do you want me to say?"

"How about something fucking useful?"

"The sun is warm. The grass is green."

"What?"

"It's some kind of Buddhist thing. The Buddhists are big around here. Why do you think I'm on this frigging pillar?"

"Are you Buddhist now?"

"I'm not anything now."

"Sheil?"

"Can you even see me?"

I can't. I can't. I can't.

THE ALMIGHTY GOOGLE

When I wake up, I crawl over to my desk and google "Gay Parenting for Dummies." That just brings up a bunch of books about how to be a gay person with kids, not what to do if your kid is gay. So I google "What to do if your kid is gay."

The first article that comes up is titled "When Your Teen Child Says He's Gay." One glance through it and my stomach knots up.

It is painful and confusing when your child claims he is gay. Rest in your faith and know that reconciliation with God is always possible. Consider:

Does your son seem confused? Is he struggling and ashamed? He may need a firmer hand.

Attraction is out of our control, but behavior is a matter of conscious, willful choice. Biblical values are stronger than the whims of the body.

Do not turn your back—maintain a godly presence in his life. Do your research, following the light of God's truth, and seek solace in the support of a Christian community. Let scripture guide your words and actions.

Does your son know Christ?

IS THIS A DATE?

Alex crashes into Stew's locker. "Hey, bro."

"You're going to give yourself shoulder damage if you don't learn to put the brakes on," I tell him.

He laughs and leans harder into the metal. "You jump a mile, like, every time. It's pretty hilarious."

"You're insane."

Alex grins. "That's what makes me crazy."

My face twitches involuntarily. All attempts to shut it down completely fail.

"There we go." Alex claps me on the shoulder. "I like to see you smile."

"I'm laughing *at* you, not *with* you," I remind him.

He shrugs. "Either way. So, are you catching the bus or is your mom picking you up?"

"No bus," I answer, to avoid an actual lie.

"Well, we can at least walk out together." He waits while I finish rummaging in my locker, regaling me with every glorified detail of the latest Cindy encounter.

In addition to his school bag, he carries one of those not-quite-canvas-but-not-quite-plastic sacks with a drawstring that forms shoulder straps. He's waving his arms as he talks, as usual. The back sack swings upward, carrying with it a wafting cloud of sweat-stink.

"Whoa, that is ripe." I bat it away with one hand and plug my nose with the other.

"Yeah," Alex says, a touch overenthusiastically. "I'm taking my gym clothes home to wash. It's been a minute. As you can tell." He laughs.

"I probably should do that, too."

"No doubt."

We start walking toward the gym. Matt has gym class last period. Maybe I'll just meet him there instead of out front.

I don't know what Matt will do when he sees me with Alex, though. If he'll come up to us, or wait until I'm alone. I kind of hope he comes up to us. That would be an easy way to get it all out in the open. But my pulse speeds up at the very thought.

"Okay," Alex says outside the locker room door. "Do you want me to wait for you?"

"Nah." All the breath rushes out of me. I shouldn't be so relieved. "Aren't you trying to catch your bus?"

"Yeah," he says. "See you later."

EYEWITNESS

The sound of gym lockers slamming is punctuated by a groan followed by laughter. A cloud of guys' voices and the rustle of movement comes from the next aisle over.

Richie Corner (of the nice ass) and a few of his pals stand in a half circle around Matt. He's pressed face-first up against the lockers with his arms twisted up behind him.

At least, that's what I thought I saw. I blink in surprise, rounding the corner, and suddenly the guys are all looking at me, and Matt is shaking out his arms and saying "Oh, hi."

"Catch you later, rimmer." Richie shoves Matt's shoulder and surges past him. His cronies follow suit.

"What are you doing in here?" Matt says when they're gone. "You're supposed to meet me out front."

"Gym clothes. Need to wash them." I eke out the few words I can manage, holding up my little bag. "What's going on? Why is your lip cut?" I ask him.

He touches the sore spot with his thumb. "I'm okay," he says. "Now that you're here." He comes closer. "Let's get out of here."

"Wait." I reach for his arm, but he pulls away.

"Not here. Just forget it, okay?" He's angry.

"Did they hurt you?"

Matt shrugs. "They like goofing around."

"It looked—"

"Those frigging jackholes," he says. "What do you want me to say?"

"Have you reported them?" The school has posters about the anti-bullying policy everywhere.

"This isn't an after-school special," he snaps. "Lay off me, all right?"

His tone is firm enough that I do. Whatever's happening between us, I don't want to blow it by being too much of a nerd. He sweeps out of the locker room, marching toward the exit doors at a fast clip. I have to kick into high gear to keep up.

"Yeah, sure. Sorry."

Matt might want to pretend like it didn't happen, but it's not that easy to forget what I saw. Or, what I think I saw. The cut on his lip is real even if my perception of the situation is flawed.

We burst out the front doors into the parking lot. Matt throws his arms out to the sides like Tim Robbins at the end of *Shawshank*. Finally free. He grins at me, carefree demeanor restored, as if the last five minutes were nothing but a brief glitch in the software.

"Turn that frown upside down, Sanders," he says. "The afternoon is ours."

He's beaming like a small child and spinning like a top, his backpack dangling from an elbow. I can't help but laugh at the picture he makes. "Where to, maestro?"

"Right now, what I want is to introduce you to the greatest sport known to teenage kind."

THIS MIGHT BE A DATE

It's our first time hanging out entirely on our own, not by accident and without the rest of the Minus-One Club. If it wasn't for the whole Matt-still-thinks-I-like-girls aspect, I'd say this might be a date.

"This is exciting," Matt says. "I haven't played with a laser tag virgin since I *was* one." He winks.

It's wishful thinking to imagine he's really talking about something else I'm totally new at.

"Glad I could help out," I answer. "You're going to have to show me all the ropes."

"Ready for ropes already?" he quips. "Down, boy." His eyes sparkle and he's clearly expecting me to laugh with him, but it takes a second to catch up to what he's joking about. Ropes? A flash of memory from a movie on cable crosses my brain. Ropes! Maybe he means the way some people tie each other up when they . . . My heart skips a beat. *Is* this a date? Are we on the same page, after all?

My phone buzzes.

Everything you need for the salad is in the fridge, Mom texts. *I'll come get you at 4:30.*

I have to stare at the message for a minute before it clicks.

"Shit."

"What?" Matt glances sideways at me.

"I forgot— Shit. I have to go home for a minute. Sorry." Double shit. Triple.

"No big," he says. "Laser tag will always be there." Matt hangs a left at the next intersection, pulling a tight U-turn. "Is something wrong?"

The laugh slips out of me like a burst of sparkling light.

"For certain values of wrong," Matt corrects. "Wronger than the usual wrong? More wrong than the fucked-up status quo? You feel me?"

"No," I manage to say. *I'll never be able to feel you, and that's the wrongest thing of all.* "Nothing's wrong, I just forgot it's Thanksgiving week already. I have to make this salad."

Matt nods, as if it's totally normal to blow off a laser tag date with a hot guy to make salad. "A salad. Okay."

"I can't—" I shake my head. I can't say any more about it for the moment.

The Monday before Thanksgiving is always the youth group Thanksgiving celebration. Sheila and I always brought this salad thing that everyone loved. I have to go home now and make it, without her. The gut punch of that is harsh; it takes my breath away.

It's in me to blow it off, to say fuck you to the whole concept of thanks, giving, and youth group. But I'd also be saying fuck you to Sheila, who loved this goddamn salad and bringing it every goddamn year. It was literally on her list of things she made me promise to do when she left for school in August. That I would still make the fucking pink salad. *Don't ruin our thing, okay? Because people expect it.*

"It's cool," Matt says, ferrying me toward home. "Whatever you need. We can rain check."

I tip my head back, staring at the visor, as if I could look right through it, right through the car roof, through the sky and the clouds, through the atmosphere and past the sun and stars, to meet the very eyes of the God I fear exists.

And who clearly hates me.

Cockblocked by the Lord, Jesus Christ, little bro? Sheila's laughing. *Serves you right.*

One day. One maybe-it's-a-date. One new memory, untied to everything from before. That's all I was hoping for here. Nothing more. I can't even have that much?

I hate you, too, I think, toward the God I'll never see.

I'm not going to *do* anything. How could I? And if you can go to hell just for your thoughts, then aren't we all already damned?

SALAD-MAKING

At first, I won't get out of the car. I'm supposed to. We're in my driveway and the house is right there, and it's embarrassing how long this moment is stretching out, but I can't make myself move.

We sit for a while, then Matt says, "Well, I like salad."

He cuts the engine and comes inside with me. It helps. In between cutting up the Jell-O, gathering the rest of the ingredients, and tossing it all into the big bowl, I manage to explain the issue.

"It'll be my first time back at youth group. But Sheila made me promise."

"You're rocking it," Matt assures me. "You got this."

I text Mom that I have a ride to youth group.

Have fun, she texts, with a little turkey emoji. Mom is very emoji-happy. She's trying a little too hard to seem chill at the moment, but I can live with it. She *is* putting up with my need to go places without her, and I won't look a gift horse in the mouth.

We sample the salad. It's okay, I guess. Passable.

"This is great," Matt says. "Never had anything like it."

I nod, wordless, but the truth is, Sheila made it better.

WINGMAN

On the way up the sidewalk from the church parking lot, Matt trudges alongside me, his hands in his pockets. I'm confused. I thought he was just going to drop me off, but here he is walking in with me. But he can't. I don't know that I can hide a lot from God, regardless, but bringing Matt to church is pretty much a neon sign screaming out my impure thoughts. God would have to be oblivious not to notice my heart pounding, the flushes of heat that his every look sends over me. I might well be struck dead if I walk across the threshold with my actual crush in tow. I can't do that to my parents right now.

A few steps shy of the door, somehow I lose the ability to put one foot in front of the other. "I don't want to go in there."

Matt stops. "So, we skip it," he says. "Tragedies happen. Maybe they don't get to enjoy the salad this year, without Sheila."

Hearing her name in someone else's words again feels strange. Good and bad all at once.

"Maybe."

"Or maybe we toss the salad onto the table real quick and bounce. Laser tag is still an option."

It's not an option. Not for me. Not tonight.

"I don't think I'm up for laser tag," I say. Making the salad and getting my ass over here pretty much took it out of me.

"That's cool," Matt says. "Anyway, I can tell this is important to you, so let's go in."

"Yeah." And yet my feet aren't moving. We're inches from the door. It could open at any moment. Someone else could come up behind us and need to pass. I'll have to introduce Matt to everyone. The handful of kids from church who go to my school are going to know right away who Matt is. And *what* Matt is. He's famous.

Anxiety quickens my breath. We can't walk in there. But how can I tell him without ruining everything?

"Or, maybe you need something to distract your mind," Matt says. "A game."

"What kind of game?"

Matt moves closer. Close enough to make my heart skip. Close enough to make me glance around to see who else might be arriving. "We're gonna walk in there and people are gonna say all kinds of inane shit, right?"

I nod. No way out of it now.

"Right, and we're going to respond. Calmly and politely."

I nod. Maybe the worst they'll think is that I've recruited the gay kid to come to youth group. Maybe it's *good* for my poster-child image.

"Except, everything we say has to have a double meaning," he says.

"What?" That's an unexpected twist, to say the least. "That's not possible."

Matt makes his voice husky. "Sure it is; we can do it all night."
He winks. "See?"

"But, I can't—"

"Come on, put your back into it."

No. "That's so . . ."

"Queer?" Matt's eyes sparkle. At least one of us is having fun.

"I wasn't going to say . . . that word."

"It's not such a bad word." Matt glances up at the cross above
the door. "In most places, anyway."

That's the rub, I think, accidentally playing his game. Uh-oh.

He stacks his hands beneath his chin and gazes upon me
sweetly. "So . . . are you gonna do it with me?" He bats his eye-
lashes.

I groan. "Oh God."

Matt slugs my shoulder. "See, now you're getting some . . . er,
getting it."

We laugh. Our breath fogs in the cold twilight, two mingling
whitish clouds. It's reckless, goofy, and far too queer for comfort, but in the warmth of Matt's presence, something loosens in
me. We're over the threshold before I know it.

The lobby is quiet, but music pulses from the fellowship hall
beyond.

Matt throws his arm across my shoulders, real casual. "Hold
up. Do we need a safe word?"

"A what?" I use the question as an excuse to slide out from
under. Not here. Not here.

Matt takes the hint. "A safe word. If it's too much, and you
want to bail, just say . . . arugula."

"Arugula?"

"Yeah, but not like a question."

"Arugula."

"Exactly."

"Arugula."

"And not until after we drop off the salad." He pats my back and opens the fellowship hall door for me.

GAG ME

Matt is some kind of social guru. I don't have to introduce him once. "Hi. I'm Matthew Rincorn, the new guy," he says, right off the bat, to anyone who comes up to us.

"Always nice to see a fresh face," Pastor Ryan says, shaking his hand. "Good to meet you, Matthew."

"The pleasure is mine," Matt says huskily, every damn time, over and over, until it makes me want to giggle. No one catches his tone. It's a sea of wide smiles and compassionate eyes.

"And good to see *you*, Kermit." Pastor Ryan hugs me warmly, but I can't relax enough to lean in. I haven't seen him since the funeral, though he's left me multiple voice mails, one for each time I missed youth group. Thoughtful, caring messages at heart, with a healthy scoop of pressure on the side.

He squeezes my shoulder. "Anything you need, my man. You know I'm hip to the struggle." Pastor Ryan was born in the wrong decade. He's the millennial the sixties forgot. Every other sentence he drops a "groovy," and his whole vibe is way laid back. He's got shaggy brown hair and a thick mustache like a Vietnam vet and drives a Honda Rebel when he's not driving the church van. On anyone else it would come across as a grown-up trying way too hard to be cool, but he's like twenty-eight and impossibly fucking earnest about everything.

Three girls I've known since confirmation cluster toward me. "You're back!" They hug me exuberantly in turn.

"I made the cranberry sauce. Are you over your intense hatred of cranberries yet, Kermit?" one of them asks.

"Gag me," I answer. That one came easy.

They giggle, and Matt laughs, too. "Good one," he says.

The girls simper in his direction. Guess his appeal cuts both ways. Only a few of the kids in youth group go to our school, so despite my worries, it's reasonable that almost no one here knows Matt is out.

"Doesn't it look amazing?" says the second girl. "Do you have any idea how much work we put in?"

"I have a grasp on it," I say. Last year, I helped with the cornucopia decoration.

"The turkey is ginormous," the third girl says.

We look toward the end of the long serving table. "Oh, that's a big one," Matt says. "Looks like it's time to undo my belt."

"How are you holding up?" one of the younger guys asks me.

"It gets pretty hard." I can't believe I'm doing this.

"I'm so sorry." His attention flicks to a burst of laughter across the room. There's fun to be had elsewhere, and I'm not fun. Holidays are supposed to be about merriment, not delicately stepping around sadness. I would have thought that, too, if I was him. "Anyway, welcome," he says to Matt.

"Thanks. It's a really nice spread."

The guy looks at me for another moment. "You're strong," he says. "You'll be okay."

"Yeah, you know. Gotta push through." I paste on a smile. Beside me, Matt is grinning. I could kill him.

And then the guy is walking away.

It's bizarre. This room is full of my people. People I've known my whole life, people I've sat in Bible study with, talking about the essence of who we are or who we should be. People I've held hands with often enough to know whose skin is warm and whose is clammy. Their lives are intertwined with mine, brothers and sisters in Christ and all. We dip small pieces of bread in a communal cup and say we are bound by something larger than what we can know.

But standing here right now, I'm apart from them. As if I'm in another place entirely. The person I want to break bread with, the person whose hand I want to hold is Matt's. He's somehow drawn me closer in our fifteen minutes of friendship than anyone here has in fifteen years.

He stands at my shoulder, letting us be apart from the laughing, mingling crowd. He's not so much here as here with *me*, that much is clear. My body cries out for that moment, not long ago, when he put his arm around my shoulder, squeezing courage into my cells so I could get through this. But since we've been in here, he hasn't touched me. Because he can't. The lightning strike might rend the ceiling in two.

Still, I turn to him. He meets my gaze. My mouth opens, and there's no thought formed, but I know I have to speak. I have to tell him—

Pastor Ryan claps his hands, breaking the spell. "Groovy crowd tonight. All you cool cats, gather round and let's pray."

"I love a man who tells me exactly what to do with my hands," Matt whispers. I snicker.

After the blessing, we line up with paper plates. Pastor Ryan wields the electric knife like a light saber, *zhoom zhoom zhoom*ing his way through the turkey breast.

"Right on," he says, laying slices on each of our plates.

Then we're standing around, gnawing on turkey and sampling the sides, eyeing the pies laid out on the dessert table.

"We've missed you at youth group!" yet another friend exclaims, braces gleaming as she smiles in greeting.

"Thanks. I needed to pull out," I say. *Holy cow!* "It was the right thing to do."

"The best Thanksgiving ever! Don't you think?" She claps her hands, grinning at me expectantly.

A handful of simple answers flit into my mind, double entendres all. Instead, I turn to Matt, who's beaming.

"Arugula."

YOU-AND-ME RULES

It's too early to go home, and I'm too fried to do anything else. Matt drives us through the dusk to the back of the Target parking lot. Yesterday's snow has already melted, except for a few salty brown humps left on the grassy median where the plows deposited their loads. We sit and stare at them, beneath the anemic glow of a pole light.

My hands are shaking. Breathing in and out requires all my focus.

Matt's eyes are closed, his head leaning against the headrest, hands resting loosely in his lap.

"You wanna talk?" he says softly, at the very moment my gaze shifts from the plow pile to his face. Did he sense me turn to look at him?

"I thought we weren't supposed to talk about it."

"Nah," he says. "That's club rules. Not you-and-me rules."

A sharp stab of emotion arcs through me. Sudden stabby sensations hit me all the time lately, TBH, but this is different. This awakens something. It's a ray of sunshine, not a slice of lightning. *You-and-me rules.* "Oh?"

Matt smiles, eyes still closed. "We make our own rules."

Then there's silence because being invited to speak doesn't

actually make me able to. The roar of the highway in the near distance punctuates the stillness.

"I'm sorry," I blurt out.

"About what? I don't see anything you need to apologize for."

My hands shake. *I'm sorry that I can't talk. Sorry that you're stuck here with me. That I dragged you to church. That I'm such a mess all the time. That I'm not brave enough to take your hand. That I'm not a better person.*

"I very much want to play laser tag with you," I confess. My voice is low but I put the last of my waning energy into it, hoping he might glean that "laser tag" means a hundred different things in this sentence.

"We will," he says, cracking a lid to peer over at me. "We'll do all the things. Don't even worry about it."

HOME

Mom is cozied up in the big chair by the front window, knitting, when I come home. "Hey," she says, motioning me over. Her voice is thick, like she's been crying.

I perch on the ottoman and pretend to ignore her remnant teariness. "Hey."

"Was that Matt who dropped you off?" she asks.

"Yeah."

"Matt's in youth group?"

"No, he just came with me today."

"That's my little evangelist," Mom says, smiling.

My stomach aches all of a sudden. "It's not like that. And I don't want to talk about it."

"So how was it?" she asks gently.

"Cloying."

She laughs and rubs her nose with her wrist. "Well, I'm glad you stuck it out."

"Sure." She doesn't need to know that I didn't.

Mom puts little hats on the ends of her knitting needles. "Do you need more to eat?"

"Nah, I'm stuffed." I pat my stomach theatrically. It's what she wants to hear, not that I barely touched my plate and then we bailed. "I still have homework," I add, which is true, but it's not like I'm actually going to rush upstairs and do it.

"Okay," she says. "Let me know if you need anything."

It's a funny thing for her to say, since that's kind of our whole relationship—me being like, "Mom!" and her doing whatever after that. I guess when you hear something said enough times it becomes easy to start saying it, too.

"Yeah." My lips brush the side of her face.

She touches my cheek.

"It was weird that she wasn't there," I say. "Even though she wouldn't have been anyway. So maybe that made it kind of normal?"

Mom takes my hand. "What are we going to do?" she whispers.

For that, I have no answer.

A SPACE THAT'S OURS

During the passing window between third and fourth period, Matt sidles up beside me. "'Sup?"

"'Sup?" I echo.

He grabs my arm and pulls me into the storage closet. We're in B loop; no Ping-Pong table, just a ragged mound of boxes piled on abandoned AV carts. He closes the door but for a sliver, separating us from the rushing river of our classmates.

"What are you doing?" Being alone with Matt in the dark stillness leaves me breathless.

"Shhh," he says, his mouth close to my ear. My back is practically up against his chest, the space is so cramped.

The chatter and bustle in the hallway peaks and then ebbs. The bell rings over the last soft scrabble of latecomers sliding into class.

"We're late now," I say, not really caring.

"We're skipping," Matt says. "Don't you ever skip class?"

"No."

"You're kidding."

"No." My cheeks flush. Nerd alert.

"Welcome to a whole new world." Matt reaches past me and pushes open the door. "Come on."

He leads me through the empty halls to the locked access stairwell that leads to the roof. He keys his way through the door.

"How do you have a key for that?" I ask.

"Got friends in high places," he says. "Or low places, depending on how you look at it." He winks. What, did he bribe a custodian or something?

Patrick and Celia are already on the roof when we emerge into the crisp fall air.

"Hey," we say. They're huddled in a small annex between the wall that houses the stairwell and some vents or whatever. Cards out. Pennies out. I rummage through my backpack, suddenly much less embarrassed that I've been carrying my own penny stash around like a security blanket since they gave it to me.

"Where are the others?"

"Simon has a history test and Janna can't skip. She didn't say why," Patrick informs me.

But four is plenty for poker, so we play. Simon and Janna must be the conversation instigators in the group. We're pretty quiet and focused on the cards, apart from the occasional slice of banter that erupts between Matt and Patrick.

"Ouch," Matt says, laying down a high flush. "Read 'em and weep, like a tiny little baby."

"Don't worry, I know how to take a hit," Patrick answers, folding his cards.

"That's not what Emerson said," Matt quips, referring to the quarterback of the football team, on which Patrick is an offensive lineman.

Patrick grins. "So come at me. Test your theory, Toothpick. I'll snap you like I'm eating hors d'oeuvres."

Celia smiles across the cards at me as they exchange their gentle barbs. In the silence between us, I sense something real about her. I like it.

"Bell's gonna ring," she says. Wow, the time has flown.

She packs up the cards. Matt steps out of the protected alcove and tips his face upward. "You can smell the sky from here," he says, spreading his arms to the chilly breeze. "I love to be high."

Patrick rolls his eyes. "Oh, we know."

Matt frowns at him. "The point is," he says, looking right at me, "it's nice to have a space that's ours alone."

THEN: BLANKET FORT (FIVE YEARS AGO)

The fort is a thing of beauty, Sheila and I agree. Couch, end table, armchair in a triangle, draped and lined with every blanket we can find. We stuff it to bursting with pillows and snuggle down. It's quiet and warm. We watch videos on Mom's tablet until the battery blinks red.

Sheila stretches, then hugs the long pillow between us and kisses it with a loud, melodramatic smack. "Why are you so cozy, you down-filled monster?"

"You're weird," I inform her, not for the first time.

"Didn't you know there are girls who kiss pillows?" she says, laughing.

In the late-afternoon shadows of our private fort, it feels safe to answer with what is really on my mind.

"Did you know there are boys who kiss boys?" I whisper in one breathless rush. "Isn't that gross?"

"All kissing is gross," Sheila says, rolling toward me. "It's super weird that people do that, when you think about it."

"Yeah," I say, inexplicably disappointed that she missed the point.

Sheila touches my cheek, still baby-full and soft. "Want to know a secret?"

"Yes." I want to know every secret in the world.

"It's okay for boys to kiss boys, sometimes."

"That's not what Pastor Rick says." We had a whole lesson on it in Sunday school, this thing I'd never heard of that now I can't stop thinking about. This thing that is bad and wrong and sinful also makes my tummy feel funny in a way that I like a little bit.

Sheila rolls back to look at our ceiling of blankets. "I know. But he isn't always right."

That idea blows my mind. I don't even know what to do with it. Jesus is the way, the truth and the life, and Pastor Rick is the closest thing we have to the voice of God. "How can he be wrong?"

"I think you'll understand when you're older," Sheila says. She's fifteen. I'm eleven. And worlds apart, apparently.

"Do Mom and Dad know about this?"

Sheila smiles. "Mom and Dad aren't always right, either," she says. "But don't tell them I said so."

My chest fills with a mix of elation and confusion. "Okay," I answer. Keeping secrets is a thing I'm very good at.

NOW: LIVING ROOM

The living room is cold and still. Stiller than it's ever been, somehow. Blankets neatly folded over the couch. Glass coasters stacked on the end table, beside a framed photo of Sheila and me as babies. A vase on the coffee table that didn't used to be there, empty. There are breakable things all around us now, I realize, that were never there when we were younger.

No one's home. There's no real reason to tiptoe. But I do.

WE GATHER TOGETHER

Real Thanksgiving comes and goes in a blur of turkey, pie, and football. My cousins who live three hours away take me under their collective wing, pulling me down onto their big L-shaped sofa and distracting me with video games and YouTube nonsense.

It's nice, and not. We go way back, but they're also full of psalms and platitudes and much of the time I can barely keep my mouth shut not to scream.

"God has a plan."

"Things happen for a reason."

"We miss her, too."

"Let God be your strength."

We pile on the couch to watch *Home Alone* and officially kick off the Christmas season.

Happy T, Matt texts around the time Macaulay Culkin is smacking Joe Pesci in the face with a frying pan.

You too.

Video chat, he writes. *One hour?*

Midnight?

Yeah. You in?

IN.

CLUB TOAST

"Boy-ooo! Sanders has entered the chat," Simon bellows when I log in at five after midnight. Matt had sent me the link but it turns out they're all there.

"Now we can toast properly," Janna says.

"Oh, hey." I didn't realize this was a whole meeting. "'Sup, y'all?"

And then I don't get another word in edgewise for nearly forty minutes. The club is in rare form tonight. The mood is downright ebullient. We're all away from home with extended family, except Celia, who's home with her parents. And it turns out that Simon's extended family is really his foster parents' family, and that has to be weird. Maybe it's him we're gathering for tonight. It's unclear. And it doesn't matter.

"Wait, wait, wait," Patrick says to Celia at one point. "Are you telling me you made fifty fired pieces this semester alone? Fifty?"

"Yeah," she says, panning the camera around her bedroom to show off her clay works. She has a shelf of wonky mugs, and another of what looks like vases. A few bowls, a couple of abstract sculptures, and a stack of not-quite-flat coasters with cool carved designs. Everything very glossy and colorful.

"Oh my God," Janna says. "It's a wonder that we ever see you."

"That's so cool," Simon adds. "How long does it take to make one?"

"Depends," Celia explains.

"Are they wonky on purpose?" I ask, eyeing the mugs.

Everyone cracks up, including Celia.

"Way to be supportive, Sanders," Patrick chides me.

"No, they look great, I mean—I like them—" I flounder to cover my gaffe.

Celia grins. "Some of them, yeah," she says. "I like asymmetrical things. Also, I'm a beginner. It's harder than it looks."

"I knit," Simon informs us, holding up a thing he's apparently been working on the whole time we've been on the call. "Also harder than it looks."

"What is it?" Janna asks.

"You can't tell?" Simon laughs. "It's a hat. Or, it will be, someday." Currently it's about the size of a teacup.

Simon has this suite of internet-based board games we can play from a distance. It's goofy and fun and perfect for blowing off steam at midnight after an awkward Thanksgiving.

At my family dinner earlier we all had to go around and say something we're thankful for. It makes me self-conscious in the best of times. Today, I dug myself out of my head long enough to say "I'm thankful for my friends," and at the time it was hella perfunctory. But now, looking at the five squares with their smiling, bantering faces, the truth hits hard. I *am* grateful. I'm grateful for this.

PRIVATE PARTY

Afterward, I text him: *When you said vchat, I thought you meant just us.*

My phone immediately vibrates with a request to chat. I pop my headphones back in.

"Hey."

"Hey."

"What's good?"

"Not much." *Seeing you.* "The game was fun. Do you always do that on holidays?"

Matt shrugs with his lips. "When we can. If we feel like it."

"How's your Thanksgiving?" I ask.

He raises a finger. "Turkey coma, party of one."

We laugh. He's at his grandparents' house in Michigan. The decor looks ripped out of the eighties.

Matt sips from a large mug shaped like a turkey. The beak and its beady little eyes rise up in the camera view, with a hint of tail feathers in the back.

"Wow, that's . . . a piece of drinkware." It feels like I'm grinning like a fool.

"Just a little holiday cheer." He raises the mug to me, turning it around so I can get the full effect. "Cheers."

"Cheers," I echo. "How did we not mock you for that mug in the group chat? That should've been a dominant thread."

Matt grins. "I was careful to hide it. I know how y'all get."

"Clever boy." I do the voice as best I can. Maybe he gets the *Jurassic Park* reference, maybe he doesn't.

"When are you home?" he asks, a yawn slipping in. "Sorry, I'm wiped."

"Tomorrow. You?"

"Saturday night." He drains the mug and rests his head against the plaid-striped cushion behind him. "Can't come soon enough."

"So . . . see you Monday?"

Matt yawns and winks. "If not sooner."

RIP

In the dream, we're floating on a broad white fluffy cloud. Crystal clear air around us, infinite miles of nothingness.

Sheila says, "Don't fart. You might burst the bubble."

"Shut up," I say. "I'm not like that."

"Dude," she says. "You can totally rip one."

"Dude," I echo. "So can you."

"Shut up," she says. "I'm a lady."

The glare I shoot at her could wither our cloud. "You can't lie to me. We share a bathroom."

"Not anymore," she says.

"Long enough, though."

"I can't fart in the dorm." She sounds wistful. "I mean, not as freely."

"Now that you live with girls, you mean?"

"I guess. People I want to be friends with."

"Your farts can be pretty foul."

"Shut up. At least mine don't sound like thunder."

"A loud fart is a good fart," I inform her. "I don't go in for the silent-but-deadlies."

She shrugs. "Smelt-it-dealt-it is a load of crap. That's for sure."

"If you have a load of crap, why are you farting anyway?"

Sheila narrows her eyes at me. "This has gone on too long. Farting is not a thing to discuss theoretically."

I smack my fist into my palm. "You wanna go?"

"Hell yeah."

"Anytime, anywhere."

"Right here, right now," she says.

"Loudest fart?"

"And smelliest. Scale of one to five?"

"Scale of ten."

"Someone's feeling ambitious."

"I've been to middle school. You ain't got nothing on me."

"Three, two, one . . . Rip!"

We both fart as hard and loud as we can. I clench my fists and bear down like I'm dropping a deuce. It does sound like thunder, and in a matter of seconds the air smells like a gas leak, as it were.

"Eww," Sheila says, fanning her nose. It's not clear who won.

"Best of three?" I say. We rip, and rip.

Beneath us the cloud grows bigger and bigger, until we realize. All this time. We're standing on a cloud of our own farts.

"Oh damn," Sheila says. "That's foul."

I jump. The fart cloud bounces me like a trampoline. "Jump," I tell her. "It's awesome."

She does. We bounce and flip and bounce some more. The laughter starts low, as low as the fart place in my gut, and spills outward. Sheila reaches across the crystal void and grabs my hand. We turn hysterical. We fart as we jump and the cloud gets higher and higher. We soar. The blank sky gives way to a starry night and we hang there, clear up in the atmosphere, just us and our farts and our laughter.

WAKE UP LAUGHING

I wake up from the dream laughing. I cover my mouth because it's wrong, all wrong. She's gone, and I'm laughing. Can't stop. Can't. Stop. Press my face into the pillow. Try not to breathe, but then the laughter just clogs my chest until my heart throbs on the verge of exploding.

It's Sunday. Four in the morning. So say the glowing clock numbers.

Matt says he doesn't sleep much. Let's test that theory.

Oooh, says Sheila's voice. *You* like *him.*

"Bad dream?" he asks after the second ring.

"No, a good one."

"That's worse, isn't it?"

I love that he knows.

"What was it about?" he says.

"I can't tell you."

"Wanna go hiking in the morning?" Matt says.

It's already morning. And it's November. But it's Matt. "Maybe in the afternoon."

"It's better in the morning," he says. "Crack of dawn."

"I didn't sleep well."

"Me either. All the more reason."

"I guess."

"I'll come get you at six," he says. "Dress warm."

"Are you serious?"

"Yeah, I was gonna go then anyway."

There's no way my parents will be up by then, on Thanksgiving Sunday. I can sneak out.

"We were laughing in the dream," I whisper. "And then I woke up."

"It could be worse," he says.

I don't see how. So I just lie quietly and listen to him breathing.

"I forget how it sounded," he tells me.

"What?"

"My mom. The sound of her laugh."

What do I say? Sheila laughs in my head so much of the time. Laughs with me. Laughs at me. Just laughs.

"See you at six," I say. "I'll be waiting out front."

"See you," Matt says.

WHERE THE
GLACIERS STOPPED

"There's a place I want to show you," Matt says, first thing. We drive out of town, out among the rolling hillsides. We're headed south, past the point where the glaciers stopped carving the land flat. Even if you don't know that the glaciers are the reason, you can feel it happen. Gradually the earth gains texture and we're no longer surrounded by fields and endless flatness but rolling hills and lush forest.

About twenty minutes later, Matt drives us into the state park and winds along the roads to a pull-off near the start of a trailhead.

The woods seem sparse. Bare-limbed trees, whitish air, low scrubby bushes with frosted leaves.

"We're really hiking?" I ask. "It's like forty degrees."

"Downright balmy," Matt says. "Your face. You look like I'm trying to take you out in a polar vortex."

"My people come from Georgia," I say. "We like things warm."

"Trust me. I won't let you freeze."

"Fine." We're here now. I'm committed. At least it's something different and unexpected.

We climb out of the car. Okay, it's not *that* cold.

Matt hefts a large backpack out of the back seat and hands me a thermos to carry. "Let's climb."

TOP OF THE WORLD

The hike is short, the air brisk. There's something calming about the living stillness of the woods. A light breeze is enough to set the branches rustling. The air smells clean and earthy, like a pile of fresh-raked leaves.

We emerge from the trail onto a small expanse of bare rock, sparse with grass and loose stones. Above us, the branches thin and the sky broadens. Maybe ten yards ahead, a small ridge of rock about four feet high juts up like a wall. We walk toward it, then Matt leads me to one side, where the ridge slopes more gently. A half dozen jagged rocks mound, forming enough footholds to climb up. Matt goes first, then reaches for my hand.

Glove in glove, he supports me as I climb. "Here we are," he says. "Top of the world. Or, at least, as close to the top as we can get in Indiana."

On top of the ridge, the hilltop is flat. We walk out a few yards to take in the view. We're on a sort of oval plateau, looking down into the valley formed by the hills of the state park. On three sides, the drop is similar to what we climbed, about a four- or five-foot drop back down to trail level. On the fourth side, it's a full-on cliffside, plunging a couple hundred feet to a blanket of trees below. It feels like we are standing on the top tier of a cake. I picture us as two little tuxedoed figures.

Getting a little ahead of yourself? Sheila muses. *Maybe try holding hands without gloves on before proposing?*

Matt walks right to the cliff edge. "Come look."

We stand side by side, taking in the view. In summer, it's probably a gorgeous green carpet, and now it looks like somebody threw down a game of pick-up sticks. But it's striking. In the distance flows the snaking line of a river. Once I get my bearings better, I'll figure out which one. The newborn sun casts pinks and oranges and purple bands along the horizon, behind the clouds.

"What do you think?" Matt asks.

"Top of the world. Definitely."

POETRY

Sheila and I used to read Shel Silverstein poems out of this book called *Where the Sidewalk Ends*. I liked to think we lived where the glaciers ended, to imagine us sitting on a cliffside at the edge of the world. Now here we are, Matt and me, which is its own kind of poetry.

I can dig it.

FLYING

"Now for the best part." Matt walks away from the cliff edge, toward the right-hand side of the plateau. He tugs a thin plastic tarp out of his pack. "This is my favorite thing," he says. "Watch this."

The tarp is large and unwieldy when it unfolds—almost the size of a twin bedsheet and the same rectangle shape. The short edges are gathered and duct-taped into something resembling handles. Matt's hands slide into the silvery slots in a familiar way; the tarp billows out behind him like a fallen cape.

He carries it like that to the edge of the rock face, and gazes down the slight four-foot drop. "It's like flying," he says. "Check it."

He flings his arms upward and leaps forward, into the air over the drop-off. The tarp catches the sky, an invisible updraft. Matt floats. Down, down, till his sneakers touch earth again. It's over in seconds, at which point I let out my breath.

Matt turns around, grinning. He calls up to me. "You wanna try?"

I shake my head.

"You'll love it," he promises. "You've never felt so free."

"Um . . ."

"Trust me," he says. "It's a religious experience."

He sounds so earnest. It makes me want to laugh.

"Close your eyes when you jump," he says. "It makes it feel like you're falling forever."

A RELIGIOUS EXPERIENCE

I'm floating. I'm flying. Weightless and free, for two long seconds that feel like eternity. In that suspended, breathless moment, there's nothing. No thoughts. No fear. No worries.

Then my feet touch down and I tumble to the earth.

How long I'm on my knees before his hand is on my shoulder, I have no idea.

Matt grins down at me. "Want to go again?"

WE INTERRUPT THIS PROGRAM FOR A PARENTAL BULLETIN

At first, the angry buzzing of my phone doesn't register. My whole being is vibrating with the intensity of being with Matt, of flying. He's taking his turn when I notice it going off. Half a dozen missed calls from my parents. Crud.

> *Where are you? We are leaving for church in ten minutes. WHERE ARE YOU?*

> *So?*

> *So, it is time for church.*

My phone rings. There's enough defiance in me to punch DECLINE.

> *Reception is not good here.*

Where?

Where I am.

Kermit.

What Matt said about the leap being a religious experience sticks with me.

I'm exploring spiritually in another way this morning.

Kermit. Home. Now.

By the time I'm there, you'll be at church.

I don't have to. They can't make me. They have no idea where I am, and it's not like they're gonna report me missing and send the cops after me.

I don't have to go back at all. Some people do it, I know. Leave and never come home. Run away and never have to explain themselves to anyone who wouldn't understand. Disappear.

"What do you want to do?" Matt says.

"It doesn't matter what I want."

I don't know why they have this power over me. Why them telling me what to do makes me do it. The consequences I fear are nebulous, just a blur in the back of my mind. And yet, it's ruined now. This perfect place and moment.

"I have to go home." Maybe because I'm not brave. Maybe because I'm a realist. Maybe because the devil you know beats the devil you don't. Regardless, I'm tethered to this misery. Falling, but without a parachute.

THE LAST STRAW

They set a family meeting for one o'clock and I don't come down. So they come up.

"The best thing we can do right now is try to keep our normal routines," Dad says.

Normal. The word, the concept, hovers in my brain like a piece of abstract art. Interesting. Captivating. Meaningful and meaningless all at once.

Routine. We have new routines now. A standing order for tissue boxes to be delivered weekly. One of us opens the freezer around dinnertime and decides which ambiguous foil package to stick in the oven. Mom cries in the bathroom every morning and every night. Dad plays Jenga with the stack of unacknowledged condolence cards on the kitchen counter. For the life of me, I don't know why they aren't balled up in bed 24-7 like I would be if I was in charge.

"I'm not too happy with God right now." It takes all I have to speak the words aloud. "Can't you just leave it alone?" Leave *me* alone?

"Church isn't about happiness," Mom says. A truth already written on my bones.

"In this family, we have certain beliefs," Dad begins.

"Shut up," I snap. It shocks them. "This family is different now. Everything is different now!"

A hot rage surges through me. Maybe I've been lying to myself. A month ago, I could go to church every goddamn week and put on a self-denying smile. I could even enjoy it. So why can't I now? Maybe it *is* because of Sheila. Maybe this was the last straw, God!

Regardless, it's much easier to stand firm when *they* think they know the reason. When *they* think they know why my heart is raging against this particular machine.

The silence stretches out for a time. Finally, Dad speaks. "If we can't turn to God in this time of grief, where can we turn?"

"Nowhere, Dad." I roll away, so I don't have to see what my words do to his face. "That's the whole fucking problem."

THEN: SHEILA'S BEDROOM (TWO YEARS AGO)

"Sheila?" I **perch** on the edge of her bed.

"Hmm?"

I take a deep breath and push the question out. "What would you do if one of your friends thought they might be gay?"

"I don't think I'd do anything," she says. "Why? What do you think I should do?"

"I mean, would you stop being friends with them?"

"No," she says.

"Would you try to help them?"

"Sure."

I breathe. "The church recommends these centers, where people can go to get help for things like that."

"No," Sheila says. "I mean, I know that, but no, I wouldn't try to change my friend. I would help in other ways, if they needed it." She turns to look at me. "I would tell them I was glad they trusted me, and that they could count on me."

"Oh. Okay." Her response is different from what I expected, and very different from what I feared. We're now further into this topic than I expected to get, and I don't know where to go from here.

"Do you want to tell me what this is about?"

I do and I don't.

"Kerm," she says into my silence. "It's okay that you like boys."

"What? No I don't." My heart thumps like its drummer took a hit of speed.

"I'm not going to tell and I'm not going to do anything," Sheila says.

I stand up and I'm suddenly two steps closer to the door. "Why—why would you think that? No I don't." That's twice. If I deny myself three times, will I be crucified?

"You already told me," Sheila says. "Remember, that day in the blanket fort?"

"I told you?" I say, struggling to remember. "But I didn't even know then."

"It wasn't what you said, it was the way you said it." She tilts her head, as if drawing up the memory. "I told you, you'd understand when you were older. And now you do."

"I guess."

"Come here." Sheila motions me toward her. I trudge toward the desk. She grabs my shirt front and pulls me down, then kisses my cheek. "I love you, frogman. Now go be gay in your own room. I have homework to finish."

NOW: SHEILA'S BEDROOM

The door is closed and it's an exercise in attention control not to glance at it every time I pass through the upstairs hallway.

I trace the line of a crack in the baseboard to avoid having to look (for the millionth time) at her penguin cartoon, her BEHOLD, MY MESS sign, the taped-up fortune cookie messages she favored.

Before, these decorative things were so familiar as to be invisible. Now, they glare at me like oncoming headlights.

YOU CAN'T DO THAT ON TELEVISION

"Hey, Kerm," Matt says into the phone. "You wanna come over?"

It's a Saturday this time, so at least I don't have to fight the powers that be about my whereabouts. And it's a relief, in fact, to know that he still wants to spend time with me.

"Sure, yeah."

We have yet to play laser tag. It's been all I can do this week to just get through each day of school. Matt's been super attentive, nodding to me in the hallway between classes, giving me a ride home every day after school, but he hasn't suggested we try an outing again, and I don't have the energy to initiate.

At home, I retreat to my bedroom as much as humanly possible, apart from the obligatory dinner appearance.

I might have been wrong about my parents not being able to stop talking. We don't talk much over the dinners. Mom tries, Dad eats like an automaton and then disappears into the den.

Falling into Matt's car and being whisked away from Griefland is a refreshing change of pace. We don't speak, either, but it's still a relief.

"Hi," he says when we're standing inside his garage, his hand on the doorknob to the house.

"Hi," I answer. Is this a thing with us? Pausing by doors to have *a moment*?

He touches my arm. "I'm glad you could come."

When he speaks now, I only hear double entendres. So I smile. "I'm glad you wanted me."

"It's like Minus-One," he says. "Sometimes I just want to be around someone who knows how it is."

"How what is?" I ask.

"Never mind," he answers.

We go inside. It's a big house, much like Steve's across the way. Living room, dining room, sitting room, den. A kitchen that gleams like the command bridge of a spaceship.

We gather snacks from a pantry that's like a walk-in closet. Then we fold ourselves away in Matt's room and let the afternoon disappear.

I feel safe here. Protected. Like I've been whisked away to another planet, where my every move isn't being scrutinized, and even if it was I wouldn't be found wanting. Even if he knew the truth, I'm certain: He wouldn't send me away.

I know how it is in my head, and my heart. But even though I'm sitting here, talking to him, and we're close, and it's just us, and it's safe, I can't really figure a way of saying it out loud.

We sit and play *Madden* and chat about nothing, and then we switch to *Mario Kart* and race through a cartoon landscape, and then we switch to an arena combat game I've never played before where we choose hunky avatars in skimpy so-called battle armor and send them to fight to the death in rotating exotic environments, and we sit there duking it out on screen until my thumbs ache but amazingly nothing else does, and the afternoon couldn't possibly get any more perfect, and then Matt goes, "Look what you can do on this," and his avatar suddenly lowers his fists and walks toward mine. My guy kind of freezes, I guess because I freeze, and Matt's guy is close now. He raises his arms, his huge muscled cartoon arms, and puts them around me, and my guy can't do anything but stand there and let him. They're kissing now, and Matt's guy has his hands in my hair, going up and down my back with his strange jerky motions. There's music in the background, new music coming from somewhere, in the game or in the room or in the back of my mind, and it's surprisingly sexy, and I swallow my fear, because it's not real, but it is real, and my real body starts straining against the fly of my jeans. And Matt whispers a keystroke and I do it and my guy lifts his arms and starts hugging him back. And they go at it, these ultimate versions of ourselves, and apart from the music and the light click of our thumbs, the room is quiet, but then comes our breathing, which gets louder, on edge.

And the fear is back now, because I don't think I can hold myself in, and my hands slip, sweat-slick, and I'm going to have to excuse myself and run, but then Matt breathes, "Don't stop," and so I don't stop, and on the screen we are locked in one another's arms, and Matt drops his head back and lets out this low scratchy moan. And easy as that, I'm going, going, gone, and it all comes out of me, into my boxers and my jeans, a hopeless mess, but it doesn't matter because it was beautiful.

And I'm not crying or anything, but it feels like I might have, in the middle of it, in the part where I became not me but this other tiny person being touched by a boy, and Matt looks at me. In the real world he looks at me, sitting on the beanbag chair on the floor in his game room, and says, "I didn't think we would take it that far," and I say to him simply, "How did you know?"

AFTERGLOW

"**The guy who** designed the game is gay," Matt explains. "He coded in special keystrokes for, you know, guys like us."

It's on the tip of my tongue to blurt "I'm not gay" like I usually do. Except that would be silly now, considering.

I pick at the tiniest ink spot on the shorts Matt has loaned me. What we just did . . . it wasn't like doing it, I know that, but it was kind of. It's harder to look at him now, although I want to more than ever.

"How did you know?" I say again, because he hasn't answered the question.

"I have reasonably good gaydar," Matt says. "I've noticed you."

"I'm not gay." It slips out that time.

He shrugs. "Okay."

"You think I'm gay?" Do other people think this? Maybe the secret isn't that much of a secret, after all.

"Doesn't matter what I think," he says. "I didn't mean to put you on the spot."

"I mean, I—" My voice sort of stalls.

Matt puts two fingers to my lips. Electric. "Shh. It's okay."

Except it's not. If Matt was a girl, we maybe could be kissing by now. As it is his fingers on my lips have to be enough, because I can't, even though we . . . I just can't.

"I'm sorry," Matt says. "I shouldn't have . . . but I really wanted to."

"Yeah." Me too.

Just kiss him, Sheila's voice says. *Give him a big gay kiss and then you can run off and have big gay babies and live happily ever after.*

"I won't tell anyone or anything."

Chicken.

"Me either," Matt says.

"I think I might be . . ." My voice trails off.

Chickenshit.

"Shh. I know. It's okay. You shouldn't have to say it until you're really, really ready to. Trust me."

I love Matt. He makes everything easy. I soften into it.

"It would be okay," I tell him, "if you, you know . . ." I put my arms up a little.

Matt smiles. Smiles in this way that's, well, it's kind of heartbreaking, actually. He slides off his bed and kneels on the floor beside me. His hands fall on my arms, right below the elbows, which are resting on my thighs.

"I love what we did," I tell him. "Thank you."

"I never did it before with anyone," he says. "Just by myself."

"I'm always by myself," I admit.

"Me too." He squeezes my arms, in the same place. I'm halfway excited again, because he's so close now.

Matt leans in and hugs me, his hands sliding up my arms, over my shoulders to my back, and he pulls me toward him and my chin tucks over his shoulder. It falls right into place like a jigsaw piece.

A SIMPLE SOLUTION

"I'm going to sleep over at Matt's house. Is that okay?" I hold my breath through Dad's responding silence.

"Let me talk to your mother," Dad says.

"Well, you know where to find me." I hang up and turn to Matt. "They're going to say no, because it's a 'church night.'"

Matt frowns. "I thought only Catholics went to church on Saturday night."

"I mean 'church night' like 'school night.' Gotta wake up and go."

"I thought you stopped going."

"It's temporary."

"Yeah?"

"Church is more mandatory than school in my house."

Matt touches the back of my hand. "That's intense."

The phone rings.

"Fuck it," Matt says. "Tell them we'll go."

"We?" I raise my eyebrows, then pick up. He waggles his brows right back at me, like a low-rent Groucho Marx.

"We'd like you to come home," Dad says. "We've been patient with your need to come back to church on your own, but if you're not going to church you need to be home. Sunday mornings are reserved for prayer and reflection, not being out with your friends."

"How about if we meet you there?" I blurt out.

Silence.

"You and Matt?" Dad says. "Meet us at church?" Repeating the latter is no doubt for Mom's sake. She's probably listening in.

"Mm-hmm."

"On time for the service?" Dad says.

Matt waggles his eyebrows, slowly leaning toward me.

"Yeah. We'll be on time, I promise."

Dad sighs, then there's a pause. "Well, okay, then. We'll take you at your word."

I hang up. "It's going to be an hour of hell," I inform Matt. "I don't know why you would subject yourself to that."

He leans in until our foreheads meet. "An hour of hell for a whole night all to ourselves?" he whispers. "Totally worth it."

MR. RINCORN, ESQUIRE

Matt knocks on his dad's half-open office door. The man at the desk has a shock of mussed blondish hair and reading glasses perched on a long, rounded nose. He's wearing a hooded Indiana University sweatshirt that somehow looks business casual on him.

"Dad, this is my friend Kermit. He's sleeping over."

It's notable, the lack of asking for permission.

"Very good," Mr. Rincorn says. "Very good." Then he looks up, as if startled. "Oh, hello, lads."

Who says lads *anymore?* Sheila laughs.

The rest of the house is neat as a pin, but the office looks like a couple of file cabinets exploded in there. It's tall piles of folders and papers everywhere, except for the small expanse of desk where he's working.

"Kermit, you say? Well, it's nice to meet you." Mr. Rincorn has his fingers between papers in the open folder in front of him. There's a tablet open on the desk as well as a desktop monitor with a massive spreadsheet displayed.

"We're gonna eat and watch a movie," Matt says.

"I'll just be another hour or so," Mr. Rincorn says. "What's showing tonight?"

"We haven't decided," Matt says. "Probably something with a lot of explosions." He winks at me and I blush.

"Very good."

"Alfredo," Matt says. "You want chicken or shrimp?"

"Whatever you're having," Mr. Rincorn says absently, his attention already back on his papers.

"Cool," Matt says, backing out of the room.

"Nice to meet you, Mr. Rincorn." I follow. "He's gonna watch the movie with us?" I whisper as we walk toward the kitchen.

"Not a chance," Matt assures me. "He always says 'another hour,' but really he'll work till he crashes."

DEFINITELY A DATE, PROBABLY

Matt cooks, apparently. He boils fettuccine and makes Alfredo sauce from scratch, with cream and butter and cheese that he had me grate into a pretty china bowl. He roasts broccoli in the oven like a boss.

"Do you like shrimp?" he asks, opening the fridge.

"Sure."

He pulls a ring of shrimp cocktail out. "In the pasta or on the side?"

"On the side seems easier, right?"

"Sold." Matt tosses the black plastic ring onto the island, where I'm sitting on one of the counter stools. "Rip 'er open."

I tug the plastic off the ring and snap the lid off.

Matt pulls out three large bowls and two salad plates. "I usually eat in front of the TV or whatever, but we could eat at the table."

"Okay."

He sets the bowls by the stove and the plates on the island in front of me, along with two forks and spoons. There's a square four-top table behind me in the bay window overlooking the backyard, which is now cast in sunset shadows.

Matt stirs the pasta, then goes behind me and rummages in the sideboard, coming up with two green-and-white placemats and a pair of short glass candlesticks.

"There should be matches in the drawer by your knee," he says, laying things out on the table. In less than a minute, I'm looking at two very nice place settings. The folded paper-towel napkins are the only thing high school about it.

He smiles at me. "What do you think?"

I'm not clear on Matt's intentions for tonight. Do I need to be?

"Looks great. Smells great. It's great, Matt." Saying his name feels good.

The timer rings. He pulls out the broccoli and pours out the pasta water. The pasta goes into the Alfredo skillet on the stovetop. Most of the broccoli goes into a serving bowl. He pulls a small container out of the fridge and nukes whatever's in it. Then he's dishing pasta into the big bowls and whisking things over to the table.

The nuked food turns out to be a piece of leftover chicken. He plops it into the third bowl of pasta, along with the rest of the broccoli.

"Matches, Kerm," he says, catching me gazing at him. "BRB." He takes the third bowl out of the kitchen, presumably to deliver it to his dad.

The matches are in the drawer where he said, next to the batteries and corn on the cob holders and a stack of three-year-old coupons. Eating by candlelight? That means something, right?

This afternoon felt like something different. Like an escalation. I mean, do straight guys watch video game porn and masturbate together? No idea. Maybe that's kind of what happens at strip clubs? I don't know. Is it a thing? Does it not mean he's into me, into me?

Matt is back. His fingers brush my palm as he takes the matches. It's everything. Ramping down my excitement might not be easy, but I have to stay realistic.

Two guys both being gay doesn't necessarily mean they're going to be gay together. I mean . . . well, that thought came out totally wrong, but that's how twisted my head feels here and now.

Is this a "first night as boyfriends" dinner, or more of a "yay, we're both gay, let's bond" kind of thing?

I'm pretty sure you can't be boyfriends with someone you've never talked about the possibility of being boyfriends with.

Christ, I'm clueless.

It's fine. It's not a date. Just a friend thing. A gay friend thing. A gay-friends-being-fancy thing. I'm on board with it.

Matt lights the candles. "Don't you think it's more atmospheric this way?"

But then he says something like that and I'm back to not knowing.

Ask him, Sheila says. *What do you have to lose?*

Um, my only gay friend?

"Yeah, great," I say.

SLEEPOVER (THE FIRST)

When the hall light clicks off beneath the door, it gets darker still. The round blue night-light allows me to see just the shadow of him.

"My dad's in bed now," Matt says. "We can do whatever we want."

"Like what?" I whisper.

"Like this." His sleeping bag shushes against the rug as he rolls closer to me. A loose flap of the bag flops onto my bare arm. I slip my arm free, raising it above my head. Matt rolls into the gap beneath my arm. His head comes to rest on my shoulder. My chest, really. His cheek lands in the soft spot over my collarbone; his breath warms the skin above my heart.

"What if your dad comes in to check on us?"

"He won't."

"But what if he does?"

"He won't. Relax."

My muscles are statue-stiff, up to and including . . . well, isn't it obvious? I mean, Matt Rincorn is lying against me. Holding me, with his arm across my middle. His elbow is right there on the band of my boxers. It's all I can do to breathe, let alone relax.

"My dad is clueless. He thinks I'm the only gay kid in the world," Matt says. "Not that you're gay or anything."

"You know I am."

"Shhh." His fingers find my lips in the dark. "You don't have to."

"You keep saying that," I mumble. "But—"

"We don't have to call it anything. I just want to lay like this."

I can't tell if he's joking with me or what. Obviously, after the video game moment, he knows. And here we are now. The warmth of his body against mine is no joke. Kermit: zero. Impure thoughts: one thousand.

"Are you mad at me? I'm sorry I ever told you I wasn't. It was . . ."

"Automatic."

"Or something."

"I'm not mad."

"I'll eventually . . . you know . . . tell people." I don't want to be one of those sad old dudes on TV who goes on a talk show and tells his wife of thirty years that he was secretly in love with her brother all that time. *But what about the children????* the wife screeches, beating him with a houndstooth sofa cushion.

Why houndstooth? It's Sheila's voice echoing in my head now. *That's weirdly specific. You upholstery freak.*

"My sister knew." My friend Alex possibly also knows, but it seems like not such a good idea to mention another guy's name right now.

"I'm glad you're in the club now," Matt says, snuggling against me. "Aren't you?"

Is there a gay club? I mean, I know there are gay clubs, but . . . oh. He probably means Minus-One.

I don't really know what to say to that. Because I am glad, and it makes me ashamed.

Matt smooths a finger over the collar of my T-shirt. "I'm not glad your sister died. You know that's not what I mean."

"Yeah."

"I'm just glad you're here right now."

"Me too."

"It's lonely at night. Thinking about everything."

"Thinking about what?"

"Everything."

"You can tell me," I whisper. "It doesn't have to be like the club."

It's quiet for a while. His head moves, and I feel his breath against my neck. I wonder if we're finally going to kiss.

HERE, WE WILL RESURRECT YOU

Our church isn't the extreme dress-up kind of church, but Matt puts on a tie anyway. We pull my jeans from yesterday out of the dryer and I wear my own clothes again.

My parents wait for us in the narthex, the foyer outside the sanctuary. They wave through the glass, with big smiles.

"*Narthex* is a weird word," Matt says as we approach.

"It's only the entryway to the weirdness," I say. "Symbolically drinking blood is a little bit weirder."

"Touché."

We climb the wide white steps and shed our coats, adding them to the row of metal hangers on the rack to our right.

"Hi, Mr. Sanders. It's nice to see you." Matt shakes my dad's hand. "Hi, Mrs. Sanders."

"Hello, Matt. Welcome to Resurrection."

Our church's actual name is the Resurrection of Christ Church, and so that's always what we say to newcomers, but today it strikes me as super awkward. Like, *here, you will be resurrected.*

"Thanks. So glad I could come," he adds, winking at me after they turn away.

"Me too. It means a lot to have you backing me up," I whisper in return, keeping my expression serene.

THE POWER OF CHRIST COMPELS YOU

The service is okay up until the sermon. Pastor Carle dons his half glasses and climbs to the pulpit. Within minutes it's clear that bringing Matt here was a terrible mistake.

"We all make choices in our lives. We all have reckless, material desires and to indulge them would lead us away from the truth we know as God."

No, no, no. Why did it have to be a sermon like this for my first one back, Matt's first one here? The weight of it all presses on me.

"Christian faith demands our strength in resisting the lures of this material world. It requires us to dig deep and find the core of our values, maintain contact with that deeper self, in the midst of all the noise, amid all the attractive and shiny baubles that fight for our attention every minute."

It isn't a sermon about same-sex desire, not explicitly, but that's all it sounds like to me. Pastor Carle's voice is urging me: *Resist. Be strong. Pretend the long, lean thigh of the boy sitting next to you isn't pressing yours gently. Pretend you didn't sleep with his head on your shoulder. Pretend your every cell isn't crying out to him even now.*

"Sin," says Pastor Carle, "is separation from God. The longer we sin, the more we indulge our base, wanton humanness, the further we get from His grace. The harder it becomes to see His light, the light of the cross, the solace of a faith community."

Solace. My eyes skim the backs of the heads filling the congregation. Would they hesitate to stone me if they knew my true heart?

Light. I glare at the pale pinkish yellow light glowing from behind the raised wooden cross above the altar. It's glaringly artificial in its neon-ness, a rectangle of bright electric bulbs. There's a knob right there in the pulpit the speaker can twist to make it brighten or dim according to the word of the moment. The glow is *not* the glow of the cross. It's theater.

"When we succumb to our sin, this solace escapes us. We fumble around in the darkness, and in the absence of God we suffer death again and again. He grieves us, until the moment we heed His call and see His light once again."

Solace. Matt's thigh against mine, keeping me grounded in this place, tethered to a reality I no longer know how to escape. One I can no longer pretend into nonexistence.

Light. The soft glint in the whites of Matt's eyes as he looks to me. Raising a brow in a way I know means *You okay?*

I'm not. I'm not okay. Not this minute. The light in me is more of a fire, a blaze catching the wind of the Holy Spirit. It's much like the can't-sit-still, my-heart-is-alight-with-something-bigger-than-myself energy that fuels an altar call. If I was faithful I might surge to my feet with my hands pressed up, as if to touch God, crying out words of commitment to His name.

As it is, I leap up and run.

COFFEE HOUR

Matt squats down in front of my hiding place. He's never been in this building before, and I'm on the second floor, outside the Sunday school rooms, under the costume rack.

"How did you find me?"

"God showed me the way."

In spite of myself, I laugh. Matt scoots around and tucks himself in beside me. The coat racks up here are low, full of kid costumes, and deep underneath. Youth group kids hide here all the time when playing sardines during a lock-in sleepover. Some of the older kids even come here to make out. Now I'm here with Matt and the irony does not escape me.

Matt leans against the bin of nativity-play props beside me. He sits silent, waiting for me to speak, maybe.

"I can't be here. I tried to tell them."

"Your sister just died," he says. "What do they expect?"

"It's not about that," I confess.

"Yeah, I know."

Sitting in this place, memories assail me. Lock-ins. The nativity play. I used to love coming to church and doing all the things. I read scriptures at the Easter service. I gave the sermon last year on Youth Sunday. I'm the youngest person ever to serve on the worship committee. I'm little Mr. Church. Ask anyone.

My head rests on my knees. I barely know who I am without a handful of Sunday obligations to be excited about. It's like a seventh of my life got erased of all meaning the moment Matt Rincorn first touched my shoulder and smiled.

Is that what makes this feeling a sin? To have encountered something so all-consuming it steals the very light of God from my eyes? Do straight people not get so completely caught up in each other?

"I get that you can't be all buddy-buddy with God with all that shit going on," Matt says.

"I used to be able to pretend. I used to try so hard to be right. To not think sinful thoughts. To *never* act on them."

My body shakes with the chill of admitting these things, in the stillness, under the coats. Strains of what must be the final hymn vibrate the floor. When the service ends, the children will come running. It's advent season, which means they'll soon be assigned their roles in the nativity play. We have to get out of here.

"Wait, how did you really find me?"

"I followed you," he says. "And once I knew where to find you, I went back to tell your folks everything was fine and you just had to go to the bathroom."

"Thanks." My forehead feels clammy against my palm. "I have to stop by the coffee hour." The thought of the grinning elders, the handclaps on my shoulder, the awkward hugs and platitudes—it's nearly unbearable.

"I'll go," Matt says. "I got this."

"They're gonna—"

Matt touches my cheek and my words disintegrate. He fishes his car keys out of his pocket. "No, really," he says. "I got it. Go wait in the car."

REFUGE

I sit in the driver's seat and blast the heater. People stream out of the reception hall in small clusters.

It's hard to imagine what Matt is saying and doing inside, with my parents, or what the fallout will be. At least maybe now they'll know that it's not best to push me.

The two halves of me crash against each other like waves against rocks, like two clouds meeting to make thunder. The part that wants to escape versus the part that wants to be normal. I wish I could be who I used to be. The kid who ran through the Sunday school halls, carefree. And I wish never again to have to think about the God who let things become the way they are.

Simple, simple, Sheila says. She always said I wanted things to be too simple. *Life's not like a jigsaw puzzle, where everything falls into place.*

All I know is that it's all too real here. It's everything I don't want to think about put together in one neat package. It's the place I spent the most time with Sheila, second only to home. It's so much a part of my life that I don't understand how to extricate, or if I can, even.

After ten minutes that feel like a hundred years, Matt hustles out of the narthex entrance alone. I loop around to the passenger side, making room for him behind the wheel.

He hops in. "Let's blow this Popsicle stand."

HAMMOCK

"**That was too** much," Matt says. We're back at his house, in the basement. He rummages in a bin and comes up with a half-full bottle of Southern Comfort whiskey.

"Sorry," I say.

"I didn't mean it like that," he says. "You don't have to apologize."

"Okay."

The basement is slightly more interesting than your average basement. It's half-finished, and full of cardboard boxes and plastic crates, like anyone's. There's a couch and a TV at one end, and a hammock on a stand randomly in the middle of everything, like the kind you'd find in someone's backyard. The hammock makes the whole space come alive somehow.

Matt opens a mini fridge by the couch and pulls out a Sprite and a Coke. He takes a long pull on the Coke and fills the gap with SoCo. He cracks the Sprite and hands it to me.

"Let's just get drunk and talk," he says, which sounds super romantic.

"I don't drink," I tell him, accepting the un-doctored Sprite.

"Really?" He hasn't forgotten. He's teasing me.

"I'm Christian," I say. "We're not supposed to."

"Screw supposed to," Matt scoffs. "No one is supposed to. That's why it's awesome."

"No thanks." I never did before and I probably never will now.

"Well, I'm going to. Like I said, today is just too much." He takes a swig direct from the whiskey bottle, then caps it and hides it again.

I shrug. It's none of my business. I'm not going to be one of those people who acts like everyone has to do what I want them to.

We lie in the hammock head to toe, with our hips right next to each other. I sip my Sprite and he sips the Coke and whiskey. It smells sweet with a little bit of a tang.

"It's not an all-Christians thing, you know," he says.

"Not drinking?"

He smiles, sips. "Well, yeah. But I meant the other thing. They don't all hate us."

"They don't hate us, just what we do." The platitude comes out automatically. I've heard it so many times.

Matt shrugs. "Same difference. When what you do comes from who you are, it's the same." He touches my fingers. "Us being here right now, like this, is not the same as us knocking over a liquor store or something."

"If we have to steal, can it at least be something we both can use?" The train of thought he's on is too heavy. Making light of it feels safer.

"What do you recommend?"

"I don't know. Candy?"

"Condoms. I bet people steal condoms all the time."

That renders me speechless. *Something we can both use.*

"Or we could always pull a bank job," he says. "Fund our dramatic island getaway."

"Is that why you have a hammock in your basement? Practicing for your life as a wealthy fugitive?"

Matt laughs. "It lives in the yard in the summer. But it makes no sense not to be able to use it year-round." He meets my eyes. "Once I get hooked on something, it's hard to let it go."

"Yeah, why is it a summer thing? Why don't more people have hammocks in their houses?"

"They do, only not around here. Some places in the world, people sleep in hammocks."

"Right." Sheila did that once, on a youth group trip to Mexico. She got so excited about it. She annoyed me for days, going on and on.

"Hammocks as beds sounds perfect to me."

Matt saying *beds* while we're hip to hip is kind of a lot to take. "And this is where we'd run to? After the bank heist?"

"We'd go anywhere. Everywhere."

We riff on the fantasy a while. Swaying. Sipping. Matt his Coke mix and me the clean Sprite.

The last of my soda goes down smooth, most of the bubbles evaporated. I tip my arm over the edge and let the empty bottle fall to the rug.

"Want another?" Matt asks, glancing toward the mini fridge.

"Nah, I'm good." *Here with you, inventing the life we'd live together if we were free.* It is perfection, a terrible aching perfection. If not for all the shadows around my heart, it might have exploded in happiness by now.

Who you calling a shadow? Sheila demands. *Don't you dare diminish me, frogman.*

It's been hard to think about Sheila lately, but impossible not to. It's been impossible to talk about her, and is hard to imagine doing so now, but also there are things that I want Matt to know. I want him to know *me*, and to know me means to know Sheila. At least, it always has before.

"My sister and I once planned a bank heist," I confide. Yet another fantasy that will never come to fruition. "Guess that's not gonna happen now, either." Not like it ever really would have, but still. Somehow I know I have to say something about how sad it is.

"Shh. Don't bring it down," Matt says. "Let's be beautiful. Let's be magic." He twines his fingers with mine.

He's right. He's right. It's better. To relax, to escape, to pretend. He's right.

Matt moves a little bit, just enough to start the hammock swaying slightly again. Our eyes are locked. He sips from his Coke.

"If I drink, will I forget about her?" I whisper. "Will it take it away?"

"No," he says. "It only makes it hurt a little less."

After a second, he tips the bottle toward me, but I shake my head. I'm scared, to be honest. If I find a thing that makes it hurt less, I might never stop.

EVERYTHING

My bladder is straining. I've held it as long as I can, so as not to break the spell. We rock in the hammock all afternoon, and I've never known such perfection.

From time to time, Matt rolls out for a minute to get us another set of drinks, then rolls back in, laces his fingers with mine, and we are where we are again. Suspended yet grounded. Still and in motion. Soothed and agitated by turns.

Any minute now, he'll get up again to refresh our drinks, but I don't know if I can wait. I don't want to be the one to end it. Matt can come and go as long as I'm perfectly still, but me getting up might change something. It might upset the balance.

However, peeing all over Matt's beloved hammock might upset the balance more. That motivates me.

"Sorry, I really have to pee," I confess, swinging my feet outward.

"In the nook behind the washing machine," Matt says. "If you need a door, you gotta go upstairs."

"Gotcha." Not having to go upstairs is a surprise, and a benefit. If our magic, suspended space encompasses the entire basement, then maybe my excursion won't break the bubble after all.

When I stand up, Matt rocks in the wake of my movement,

adjusting his weight so the hammock doesn't flip. "Ooop," he says, riding the wave. He scoots forward, swinging his legs down, then reaches for my hand to help him up. He lets the Coke bottle drop into the hammock.

"You okay?"

"Yeah. Thanks." He's standing now, and close. Still holding my hand. Face-to-face.

When I start to pull away, he doesn't let go. We stretch out like an accordion.

"Hey there," he whispers, cupping my hand in both of his and drawing me back. "Where are you going?"

"Are you drunk?" I ask. My sense of how much a person has to drink to get actually drunk is pretty hazy. To me the amount he's had seems like it could be a lot, but I don't really know.

"Nah," he says. "Just feeling good. Being here, with you."

His words thrill and terrify me.

"There's a reason they call it liquid courage," he says. He brushes a finger along my collarbone, skin to skin, through the cast-askew neck of my hoodie. My entire being falls motionless. His other hand, still holding mine, tugs me even closer, but I'm a statue it seems, so Matt is the one who moves. He wraps my arm behind him and leans in until our lips are nearly touching.

It's everything, that tiny space. It's everything, for one long moment, and then his lips close the gap and press mine.

Our noses touch. He tilts his head and pulls back a bit, then comes in again. Pressing, sipping, touching. The gap is no longer everything. The contact is.

PAUSE BUTTON VIOLATION

Time passes, with Matt's lips on mine. His hands cup my shoulders. My mouth parts, the tiniest bit—I can't help it—and he taps my lips with his tongue.

The soft sharpness of the feeling jolts me back to reality. I step back, putting an arm's length between us.

"You okay?" Matt asks, opening his eyes.

"Yeah. No."

"No? You didn't like it?"

"No! I mean, yes."

Matt pulls back, too, uncertain.

"I need a minute, is all." I rub my hands on my jeans.

"Yeah, of course." He crosses his arms over his stomach, like he's cold.

"I did like it," I clarify, moving toward him. It would be wrong to let him think otherwise.

"Yeah?" His eyes brighten and he leans back in, running his hands across my shoulders and pulling me close.

"The thing is, I still really, really gotta pee."

Matt laughs and lets me go.

COURAGE

I have no courage, liquid or otherwise. A courageous person would've done more than stand there.

The toilet is tucked into a little nook, out of sight of the hammock. I'm in there awhile, waiting for my body to switch gears and let me pee instead of being all turned on. Not sure it's gonna happen. Apparently, my penis is as confused as the rest of me.

There. Whew. It's a relief to let at least one thing go.

I wash and dry my hands at the utility sink, then lean my head against the exposed beam alongside it.

A courageous person would walk back out there and take Matt right into his arms. Can I be that person? Maybe. Maybe. Except . . .

I shake my head to clear it.

No. A truly courageous person would call upon the Holy Spirt, demand to be filled with strength to resist the lure of the devil at my tongue.

COURAGE?

Matt's sitting on the couch, waiting for me. He drinks from a fresh bottle of Coke.

Courage, I remind myself.

Walking back toward him is among the hardest things I've ever had to do. Leaving, though, would be impossible.

We sit close, side by side. I crave the simple solace of the hammock. Him there, me here, no ambiguity, no alternatives. The couch is nothing but ambiguity. Where do I put my body? Where do I put my hands?

Matt doesn't move or try to touch me. I know what it means. I confused him before. The ball is in my court, in a game I don't have the first clue how to play.

I've never been kissed. That's obvious, right?

Matt's hand is right there, resting on his thigh. My hand inches toward it, but at this rate we'll be holding hands in a hundred years.

Courage.

"Do you think kisses are like potato chips?" I say.

"Like potato chips?" Matt echoes.

"It's hard to stop after one."

SUNSET, SCHOOL NIGHT

"I **have to** call my parents soon," I say, as the sun goes down. There's only one slender, high window in the basement, covered with a light gauzy curtain that grows more shadowy by the minute.

"Why?"

"To come pick me up." I glance down at his bottle of Coke-plus. Do I have to say it? I don't want to have to say it.

"No," Matt says. "Won't you just stay over again?"

"I can't. It's a school night."

"So?"

"So . . . my parents will say no." No need to ask. Some things are written in stone.

Matt blinks. "Oh, right. Shit. I was thinking you'd want to stay."

What I want has nothing to do with it. If it was up to me, I'd stay forever, but a wish is but a shadow of a dream.

"My house has way more rules than your house apparently."

Matt doesn't make excuses or argue that he's still okay to drive. Just says "shit" again. Some rules are hard and fast and I'm grateful we're on the same page about that. I don't know how well I could have handled it if he even offered.

"Well, do you want to walk to Rallyburger for dinner? I don't feel like cooking."

"They're going to want me home for dinner." God, I feel like such a nerd. Obviously Matt has this free rein that I don't have.

I text Dad and get a thumbs-up back. Matt and I walk to Rallyburger together, because he still needs to eat and having Dad pick me up there feels one step safer, somehow.

It might have been a partial truth, what I told Matt about having to be home for dinner. Maybe that would have been okay. They hadn't yet started bugging me about getting home. And I'm hungry. But I shut it down nonetheless.

Maybe it was too much, the idea of sitting across a diner table from Matt, for the whole world to see.

IN PLAIN SIGHT

We kissed goodbye at the house, because I can't have us doing that in public. It's already a lot to be seen walking together. Kids from school are always at Rallyburger.

Matt waits out front on the bench with me.

"You can go on in," I say. "They'll be here any minute."

Matt says gently, "Do you want me to be gone when they get here?" He makes it clear with his voice that he understands if the answer has to be yes. My heart melts at the sweetness. He's had a lot to drink, but I only know that because I watched him drink it. On the outside, he seems fine. Relaxed and calm and charming.

"I'm sure it's fine," I say, though I'm far from sure.

So we sit on the bench beneath the dim sidewalk light. We put our hands flat on the bench, side by side, allowing our fingers to tease at each other where no one can see.

The fleeting thrill of danger fills me with longing. What if we could be one of those couples who walk down the hall holding hands, or make out against a bank of lockers during the passing period? But we can't.

Dad's headlights sweep over us and I jerk my hand away.

THEN: ZUCCHINI LESSONS (EIGHTEEN MONTHS AGO)

Dad comes into my room holding a zucchini and a small black plastic bag. "We need to talk."

Uh-oh.

"You're starting high school, and that means you're growing up. A lot of things are changing, including your body." He reaches into the bag and pulls out a box of condoms.

"*No*," I declare. "Dad, no. It's fine." I went through puberty like two years ago and had to sit through him talking at me about sperm and eggs. I shudder at the memory. "I know all about the birds and the bees already, remember?"

But he forges on. "In my day, we learned this stuff in school, but that's not going to happen under an abstinence-only curriculum."

"*Dad.*"

"Abstinence is still the most important thing," he reminds me. "As Christians, our faith dictates that sexual activity must be reserved for marriage." He tips his chin down, giving me a pointed stare.

I toss him a double thumbs-up. "No sex before marriage. Got it. Are we done now?"

Dad nods. "Good. But your body is capable of it now, so there are things you should know." He holds up the zucchini.

"Ew, Dad. No. It's fine. I'll wait. I promise."

"This is awkward for both of us." He hands me the zucchini and opens the box of condoms.

"*Dad*. What would Pastor Carle say?" My last-ditch effort to stop what's about to happen, though thinking of Pastor Carle in this context activates my gag reflex.

"Your mother and I believe that information is power." He holds up one square foil pouch. "Do you know what this is?"

"It's a condom, duh. I wasn't born yesterday. If I take a vow of eternal chastity, can we be done now?"

Dad laughs. "That's easy to say right now. But someday you'll meet a girl who lights things up for you, and it won't be so academic."

These are the moments. It's like the pitch is tossed and all I'd have to do is step to the plate with "or a boy" and the truth would be out there. Instead it sails past me, right into the glove. Strike.

"I'm not in a rush."

"Good," Dad says. "Girls complicate everything. You'll see."

Strike two.

"Okay, tear it open carefully," he instructs. He holds the zucchini steady and talks me through pinching the condom tip, rolling it down, and sliding it back off. I'm supposed to be picturing doing this on myself, but instead I'm picturing doing it on someone else. A series of snapshots flows through my mind. Hot young celebrities with sultry expressions, all aimed at me, maybe lifting the corner of their shirts to reveal their perfect abs.

"Good," Dad says, ruining the fantasy. He's sitting right there. So gross.

"I thought married people didn't have to use condoms," I say. "Isn't that the point?" Meanwhile, I'm thinking: Does the waiting until marriage rule apply if you're already sinning?

"It's more complicated sometimes," Dad says.

"But, mainly they're useful for people who don't wait."

"Abstinence is a choice, and it takes effort. I want you to be safe." Dad sighs. "Not everyone succeeds at it. You haven't gotten really into girls yet, but when you do, all this talk will make sense." He claps my shoulder.

Strike three. I'm out.

"What doesn't make sense is to wait until you're about to get married to talk about protection. Even though we want to emphasize that we believe in you, Kermit. We believe you won't abuse this knowledge. And knowing is nothing to be ashamed of."

Dad stands up. "Trust me, Kermit. Girls can be real temptresses, Garden of Eden style. You can't expect them to fully know what they want, or to fully understand the consequences of sex. You have to be the strong and levelheaded one."

"Dad!" Sheila shouts, bursting into the room. "Don't tell him that. That's such toxic masculinity."

Ew. She's been listening? That's extra mortifying.

"Hey," Dad says, holding up his hands. "I was a teen boy once, okay? There are some girls who throw themselves at you, as if they don't have a care in the world."

"Ew," Sheila and I say in unison. No one wants to imagine Dad as a sex object.

Sheila crosses her arms. "I think your work here is done," she says. "Kerm is gonna be fine." When Dad doesn't immediately leave, she grabs him and drags him out the door.

"God," she says, leaning her back against the door. "I'm so sorry."

"You got the condom talk, too?"

"Oh, you're not even done. You'll get Mom's version next."

"Better or worse?"

Sheila grins. "Nah. I'm not gonna ruin it for you. Where's the fun in that?"

"So helpful. Thanks." I toss a pillow at her head.

She tosses it back.

We stare at the used zucchini. "Bet you didn't consent to this abuse," I say to it.

Sheila snickers. "Nonsense." She affects the high-pitched voice of the zucchini. "I like rubber hugs."

We laugh till we ache.

NOW: AT THE READY

Can't help it. As soon as we get home, I close myself in my bedroom and look for them. Yup. The box of condoms still rests in the back of my underwear drawer, where I jammed it the day Dad gave it to me.

It occurs to me that maybe gifting these to me was his way of saying it's okay to go against the grain. Abstinence is difficult, or something like that, is what he said.

But I don't really think he meant it's okay. It's probably more like how he can talk about the effects of alcohol or drugs on the human body and expect me to take that as even more reason not to mess with them. The effect that's good is outweighed by all the effects that are bad, so abstinence is being smart about it. If you're strong enough to resist.

Temptation is all around us, remember.

The voice in my head is not Dad. Or Mom. Or Pastor Carle, or even Sheila.

"Kissing doesn't count," I say out loud. "I swear, it doesn't."

TOUGH COOKIE

In the dream, Sheila's nowhere to be seen. I look and look and look. And search and search some more.

She's close, I know. I can feel her.

But I don't have hands to put out to try and touch her. We are in a place that's empty of everything physical. It is just our intangible selves.

"Where are you?" I ask her.

"Where are you?" she responds. And when I can't figure it, she adds, "See? There's no easy answer."

"Are you haunting me?" I ask her.

"You make it sound so sinister."

"I want you back. All the way. Not like this."

"Tough cookies." She sighs. "Someone we know used to say that."

"Grandpa."

"Right, Grandpa," she says, like she'd forgotten him altogether.

"He also used to say 'you're a tough cookie.'" I want to remind her.

"Me in particular?"

"It was just a thing he said a lot. Don't you remember?"

"I remember banana splits," she says. "I miss those."

"You preferred milkshakes," I remind her.

"Yeah," she says. "Yeah."

And then she's gone again. I'm looking, looking, looking, like we're playing hide-and-seek.

She's waiting, quietly, on the swing set we had when we were small. We're too big for it, legs stretched out long on the grass, hands engulfing slender chains. "Olly olly oxen free," she says when I arrive breathless.

"Really?" I say. "This is what you're doing with your afterlife?"

"What makes you think it's my choice?"

CELIA

When the doorbell rings, I open the front door and Celia's standing there. It's a relief that it's not someone coming to express condolences. *We only just heard. How awful. *insert casserole**

"Hey," Celia says.

"Hey."

"What's up?"

"Not much. Do you live nearby?" She doesn't ride my bus, that's for sure.

"Not really." She points at the side of our garage, where a gray-and-white ten-speed leans against the siding. She names the next subdivision over. "I babysit for a kid down the street from you, so I was passing by."

"Oh. How did you know where I live?"

She tips her head, like she's searching for an answer. "I don't know," she says finally. "Must have seen you in the yard or something."

"Oh."

"I made this for you." She thrusts a newsprint-encased package about the size of a softball at me. "It's fragile."

"Thanks." I pull off the paper. It's a mug, slightly less wonky than the previous ones.

"I'm making one for everyone," she says. "Yours was the first to turn out somewhat right."

The mug is carved and painted with an image of Sheila's face. It really looks like her, too. And it's modeled after Sheila's senior yearbook photo, as opposed to the one we published with her obituary, which strikes me as thoughtful.

"It's really nice," I tell her, and I mean it. "Thanks."

"Do you want to go for a walk or something?" she suggests. "We don't have to, you know, talk or anything."

That works. It's not like I have anything better to do. "Sure."

She waits on the porch while I take the mug up to my bedroom. I tug on my tennis shoes and pull the door shut behind me.

DAZED AND CONFUSED

My parents are confused and disappointed when I once again refuse to go to youth group.

"You said I didn't have to go as long as I'm at home, not out with my friends," I remind them.

"That's not what we said," Dad insists.

"It kind of is." Mom for the win, scooping a surprise layup for my team.

Things are going my way, so there's no harm in offering a little painful honesty. I haul my miserable, pajama-clad ass upright. "Thank you. I just can't do it," I tell them, meaning it. "I wish I could be the good kid you want me to be. But I'm not. And I'm really sorry." I'm apologizing for something much bigger and they have no idea, because those are the words I can never, ever say.

Mom bustles in and throws herself at me. "We love you so much."

"I know, Mom." There's an ache behind my eyes and I badly want to close them again.

LASER TAG GLORY

Matt and I finally play laser tag, and it's perfect. Moving through the dark, side by side, taking out enemies and having each other's backs. The air is dark gray and the laser lights bright candy-colored bulbs on our chests, shoulders, and guns. It is strategic, like a video game come to life. It is the closest we will come to showing who we are to each other in public. Matt's hand on my arm, mine on his back. Shoulders touching as we try to stay together while maneuvering through the arena.

We are epic. We are heroic. We glide through the fog like action movie heroes, breathless with the nearness of each other, caught in the magic of the game.

THE MANY FACES OF GOD

I'd play laser tag every single day if I could. We go again on Saturday, and Matt invites me to stay over, but if I stay over, we'll have to go to church in the morning. Matt makes a face at the thought and I don't want to put him through that again. Lord knows I don't want to go through it myself.

We sit in the car in the Laser X parking lot holding hands and thinking about the problem. We can go hang out at my house until Matt's curfew, and we will, but at that point we can't kiss or touch or snuggle anymore.

"Their rule is you have to go to church, but do you have to go to their church?" Matt asks.

"What do you mean?"

"Sometime I could bring you to the church my mom went to."

"Your mom went to church?" It shouldn't be that surprising. Most people around here go to church to some extent.

"Yeah. She was in the choir."

"Cool." I've never thought about the possibility of another church. I don't know how that would fly with my parents. Absolutely no idea.

"I stopped going, but not because I'm gay," he says. "Our church was fine with that."

"Why, then?"

"Because all institutions are about power. And God is supposed to be about something else." He scratches the length of my index finger with his nail. Lightly, like a shiver.

"What?" I ask, suddenly breathless.

He leans toward me. "Some people call it love," he says. "But even that's too simple."

ALL ABOARD

In the dream, we are riding on a train. We can't find two seats together, so we choose aisle seats next to single travelers in the same row. The conductor moves up and down the aisle, and it stops us reaching for each other. *Keep the aisle clear.*

"Sheila." I stretch.

"Kermit." Her voice sounds distant, echoey. My heart thunders, louder than the mechanical chug of the train gears, driving us forward, faster and faster. Out the windows the landscape blurs.

My arm weighs a thousand pounds; the dream weight keeps me from moving. The aisle grows wider and wider. The tracks themselves rise up between us. Clacking and racketing, stones dancing in the railbeds. To reach might be to fall, but I have to reach. I have to.

"Sheila."

. . .

"Sheila!"

RELIEF

When I wake, I can't breathe. The dreams are supposed to bring Sheila to me, not away.

When I used to have bad dreams, it was always a worst-case scenario. A heart-racing, soul-shaking sense of terror and loneliness. But I feel that when I'm awake now. So any dream, no matter how bad, brings a measure of relief.

COURAGE, REDUX

"**It's not as** big a deal as you're making it out to be," Matt says. We learned our lesson last weekend, so now it's Friday, and I'm at Matt's house. Sleeping over.

"I'm sorry I'm not braver," I tell him. Matt wants to take me out on a date, to dinner and a movie, but I can't. I can't.

"It's not like we'd make out at the theater," he says. "You'd go to dinner and a movie with Alex, no problem, right?"

But Alex isn't gay.

"I'm not asking you to come out," Matt reassures me. "That's not a thing with me. I'm only trying to understand why you're okay with playing laser tag with me, in public, but not other things."

Something about the dark, the fog, maybe also the general stereotypical maleness of it? But I don't know how to say those things out loud.

"You make it look easy," I say. "But what we do already is a lot for me."

"I'm not trying to pretend like it's easy," Matt says. "But you think it's like this door you walk through and suddenly you're on the other side. Out." He makes jazz hands.

"It feels like that. No turning back."

"You're afraid of rumors?" he asks. "That's all we're risking, really."

Yes, because the rumors would be true. I'm afraid of the truth getting out. "I guess. I know it's kind of shitty of me." I'm basically saying I don't want to be seen in public with him. That can't be fun to hear.

"It's not," Matt says. "You deserve to be comfortable about any hint of coming out."

"I feel like I'm letting you down. Or hurting your feelings."

"Nah." He grins. "Invincible, remember?" He plops a gentle kiss on my lips, then goes to his liquor stash.

Ugh. "See? I'm driving you to drink."

Matt shrugs. "We're in for the night, right?" he says. "We can stream a movie. It's no big deal."

I follow him across the basement, put my arms around him. "I'm not ready. I'm so sorry."

"So we won't go. Honestly, it's better for you right now to keep things as they are. I get that." He turns toward me, scooping me close and hugging me tight. "This is all I need, too. It was just a thought. I've never been on a real date."

Me either. The thought makes my stomach ache with nervousness and excitement by turns. I'm denying him something he's waited a long time for, and I hate it.

"How do you turn off the part of you that's been told a thousand times that it's wrong?" It comes out like a whisper.

Matt traces my fresh-cut edges with a finger. "It's not wrong. Everything else we do in life might be wrong, but not this. Not you and me."

APPEARANCES

"**How come nothing** ever gets to you?" I ask him later. After the movie, after the making out, as we prep the pair of sleeping bags on his bedroom rug.

"What makes you think that?" he says, wriggling into his bag.

"You're so calm and comfortable about everything." He's genuinely not upset that I ruined his date plan. He's been chill and affectionate all night, while I'm over here worrying about everything.

"That's how I seem to you?" He sounds genuinely surprised.

"You're always so cheerful and brave. Like you can do anything, and be fine with it."

I scoot into my bag and Matt rolls toward me. "Well, someone has to look out for you, I guess," he says. "So maybe I have to be strong." He rests his head on my chest.

I hold him in the silence, for so long I think he's fallen asleep.

"But I don't feel any of what you said," he says. "Maybe I just don't know how to be another way on the outside."

SHOULDN'T

"You shouldn't dream about me so much," Sheila says. "I'm supposed to be someplace else."

"Well, you're here now."

"Only for now."

"What does that mean?"

"You know."

"I don't."

"You have to say goodbye eventually."

"No, I don't."

"Kerm."

"I'll always have dreams, and then I'll always have you."

"You won't."

"Are you going to leave?"

Sheila sighs. "You're trying to make a really hard thing simple."

SLEEP MAGIC

Dad is worried about how much I love to sleep. I do love it. Not because I love the dreams. The dreams are weird. The dreams are not what's magical.

You want the honest truth? The reason I like to sleep so much is that there's a moment, right when I wake up—sometimes it's long and sometimes it's fleeting—but there's at least a tiny moment when Sheila isn't dead.

Of course, there's a moment instantly after that when she becomes dead again. And that is pretty terrible. But it's worth it for that split-second feeling. When I'm not quite awake, but no longer asleep, and Sheila's alive again.

BAGGAGE

I understand what people mean now when they talk about having baggage. Unwieldy suitcases full of emotional crap you have to lug around with you.

Meatloaf says my life is a highway and my soul is the car. He doesn't mention that the roof rack is so loaded that it's putting drag on everything going forward. I don't have to look in the rearview mirror. It's all already up there, weighing me down.

ENOUGH

Dad drops me at Matt's house with pizza around dinnertime on Friday. We've done our Christmas shopping for Mom and now my reward for sonly diligence is some much-needed Matt time. He meets me at the side door, leaning out to wave to Dad as he backs out of the driveway.

"Hey, you." His cheeks are elfishly rosy, his eyes bright.

"Started early tonight?" It's a comment more than a question.

"I'm fine," he says a little defensively. "I knew I didn't have to pick you up, so what's the big deal?"

"It's okay." I kiss him, because I can do that now. "I was just asking."

He kisses me back intently.

"Did something happen?" I'm starting to understand his rhythms.

"You're here now. So everything's perfect." His hands are all over me. I've barely set the pizzas down on the island. His touch sends shivers through me.

"Where's your dad?"

"Working." He kisses my neck, my jaw. He tugs my shirt up without even trying to unbutton the collar.

"Hang on." I work the two buttons swiftly, then let him uncover me. "Aren't you hungry, though?"

"Starving." Matt's mouth catches mine. It's captivating, in every sense. But the smell of warm cheese and garlic surrounds us and my stomach growls nonetheless. Standing shirtless in the kitchen makes me feel far too exposed.

"Let's eat," I suggest, pushing at his shoulders.

"Or . . ." He grins and tries to kiss me again. I duck past his forays and put a couple of pieces of pizza on a plate for his dad. Best if I deliver it, with Matt in this state, so I slip my shirt back on and bring the plate to him in his office.

"Thanks, hon," Mr. Rincorn says, distracted. I'm honestly not sure if he thinks I'm Matt, or if he just randomly calls people hon.

We bring the other whole pizza down to the basement and polish it off in record time. Matt pulls my shirt off again. This is what we do now, and as far as we go. Shirts off, kissing with tongue. Touching. We lie on the couch, skin to skin on top.

"How much have you had to drink?" I ask him. I wonder if it will have been enough that he won't lie to me.

"Enough," he says. "Just enough."

When he drinks, his kisses turn sloppy. Is it wrong that it turns me on? How soft he becomes, and how his head lolls gently against my shoulder.

"You used to say there was never enough," I whisper.

"You make it enough," he says. "Being with you."

STRONG

There's something that happens when Matt drinks for a while. A switch that gets flipped or a window that gets opened. It doesn't happen every time, there must be some magic formula, and maybe it's weird, but I look forward to those times. I love how we escape into fantasies and games and fooling around most of the time, but it's comforting, too, to know he's trusting me with something we can't talk about in the full light of day.

We curl up on the basement couch, watching a cheesy action movie. Then he lets me tell him about Sheila, and the jokes she'd have made at the actors' expense. It's a relief, for a change, that he doesn't shut it down or try to deflect.

"All this time we spend not thinking about death," he goes. "I'm always thinking about it."

"Me too, I guess."

He's quiet for a beat.

"You're dealing with a lot," I say. "It's impressive how you handle everything."

"I don't know how much more I can take," he says.

"Of what?"

Matt shrugs, chugs what remains of his drink. He sets it aside and leans against me, resting his head in my lap and pulling my arm across his chest.

I cradle him. "You can tell me. I like knowing what's going on with you."

His arms are folded over his chest. I gently touch the exposed ring of bruises on his wrist. He pulls his sleeve to cover it again. "Don't."

"What happened today?" I ask. "You seemed upset when I got here."

"Nah. I'm invisible. Invisible." He frowns. "Invisible?"

"Invincible?"

"Yeah, that one."

"You don't have to be invincible all the time."

"It's a superpower," he says. "Sometimes I think you're the only one who sees me at all."

Hmm. "Who do you want to see you?" I ask, but I'm pretty sure I already know. There's no way I could wander half drunk around the house with my boyfriend and have it go unnoticed.

Matt shrugs. "There are worse things. Do you want to sit in the hammock?" He pushes himself up and I sense that the window has closed.

"Sure." I pull him to his feet and he leans on me, wrapping his arms around me and dancing me toward the hammock. He laughs.

All week at school and after, Matt is all smiles and sunshine, energy and escape. We glory in each other's total commitment to goofiness. It's a blur of video games, laser tag, hammock time, making out. When I stay over on the weekends, it's different. Softer. Like this.

ROCK-A-BYE

We tumble into the hammock, face-to-face. He sips at my mouth and wraps his arms around me, pulling a blanket up over us.

"Let's sleep here," Matt says. "You're staying over, right?"

It's already past midnight. He snuggles against me.

"Sleep in the hammock?"

"Are you warm enough? Are you comfortable?"

"Epically."

"So it's settled."

Fingers intertwined, we rock ourselves to sleep.

HAVEN

"I really wonder if we can move them on the church thing," Matt says when it comes time to part once again on a Saturday night. "You deserve to see what it's like to be in a place where who you love doesn't make you a pariah."

"I don't know what that's like," I say. "It's hard to even imagine." All I see around me are the ways we aren't accepted, the flaws. Matt sees it differently.

"There's a lot of homophobia in the world," he says. "But you act like it's everything, everywhere. It's not."

I shake my head. It doesn't feel real to me. Matt shows me even more movies, brochures, websites than I've found on my own. A veritable digital explosion of rainbows. It all reads like fiction.

"Some places I go online, it's like a haven," Matt says. "This weird utopia where any little homophobic thing gets called out as messed up. Kids who live in big cities, they act like the way we want the world to be is the way it really is. I don't know what to make of that."

"There are no billboards in big cities," I say. "They don't have to ride past smiling Reverend Dan on the bus to school every goddamn day."

We recite his sign in unison: "Come out . . . to church and pray the gay away!" I bare my teeth in a reasonable facsimile of Reverend Dan's psychotic grin.

"I wish harm on his dentist," Matt says. "That shit just ain't right."

"His teeth are whiter than his . . . whiteness." I'm already laughing.

"I had to post a picture of it in one of my chat groups," Matt says. "No one could believe it was a real billboard. Some of them still think it was photoshopped."

"Welcome to middle America," I say. "Land of the forcibly closeted."

Matt is a relief in this regard. People online sometimes talk about how great it is to come out and how everyone should come out as soon as possible so that the world becomes full of happy, out gay people and everyone will know a bunch of happy, out gay people and it will start seeming strange to find happy, out gay people so unusual. That makes logical sense, except then there's the newspapers, and there's always a story about a kid who's getting beaten and another who can't go to his prom and another who's living on the street because his evangelical Christian parents kicked him out and now he's a sex worker in Little Rock or Pittsburgh because he doesn't even have the money to get a bus or a train to someplace better. And then there is what-happened-slash-is-happening to Matt in our very own high school. He might not admit it, but I know things haven't been as smooth since he came out as he likes to pretend.

"You okay?" he says now.

"This moment? Yeah."

This moment, this place, is safe. It's separate from the world. We inhabit our own planet in Matt's basement. He doesn't say it, but he wants us to live on planet Earth. To walk down the halls at school holding hands and go to the movies and be something other than alone. My imagination paints the picture, but my logic brain erases it. Glorious graffiti, followed by a power washer. It's hard for me to consider even walking upstairs with my hand still in his. Because my imagination does other things, too. It paints Dad slamming doors and Mom weeping, hunched over the Bible. It paints both of them gazing at me, shattered, haunted, the way they looked after Sheila's funeral. I'd be dead to them. I imagine Pastor Carle standing over me, wielding a cross, shouting "the power of Christ compels you!" and dousing me with baptismal water like it's an exorcism.

I try to see it differently, like how it happens on TV: a few empathetic tears, a little surprise, and lots of love. But that picture is harder to paint.

Matt kisses me at the bottom of the stairs. Kissing is both the same and different from what I always imagined.

"Laser tag Monday?" This is our habit now, planning the next time we'll see each other before I leave, so that we know exactly how long we have to wait.

"Absolutely."

ALEX THE ATTENTIVE

After Tae Kwon Do, Alex catches up with me waiting for Dad. We're back to the usual pattern of his mom dropping us both off and Dad picking us up. But lately it's awkward because I'm spending all my time with Matt, and presumably Alex is spending a lot of time with Cindy. So we're not in our usual easy mode. We're at a disconnect.

"Hey," he says, plopping his gym bag alongside mine. "I feel like I haven't seen you in forever."

"I know. Sorry." Last week he made a thing about how I never return his texts anymore. Guilty as charged, and despite my promises, I've made no improvement since.

"There's a basketball game on Saturday. Season starting up. Wanna go with me?"

I should say yes, and I might've, if Matt hadn't already told me we have a club obligation in the morning, and there's no telling how long that might go, or what I'll feel like after.

I make a face. "Go to school for a sixth day in a row, you mean? Thanks, but that's a hard pass."

Alex laughs. He's the basketball fan, not me. I'm more into football, to the extent that I'm into any of it. "Fair enough. But we should do something. Soon."

"Yeah," I agree, feeling vague about the whole idea. I'm always so tired.

"Yeah," he says.

And then I'm saved by Dad arriving to get us.

ANNIVERSARY

Certain things about the Minus-One Club remain cryptic. Unclear if that's by design, or if it's all simply kind of haphazard. Matt has me block off a three-hour window over lunchtime on Saturday for "club business." Exactly that nebulous. No further explanation.

The drive soon becomes familiar. "What is this about?" I say, not liking the trajectory.

"Just a little errand," Matt says.

The discomfort in me grows. "No. I don't want to go."

Matt glances at me. "What's wrong? It's for the club. We have to."

"At the cemetery?"

"How did you know?"

My breathing shallows. I don't answer.

"Oh," Matt says. "Shit."

"I don't want to go." My reaction is surprising even to me. Maybe I should want to go? We're not a visit-the-grave kind of family, or at least, we're not right now. Sheila isn't there. Not really. That's what we believe.

"We're not going in," Matt says. "We can wait at the gates."

The gate sounds bad enough, but I can live with it. I don't

want to walk the grass or see the stone. I don't know if I never will, or if it's just too soon. "Wait for what?"

"For Celia. We celebrate anniversaries," Matt says. "When we want to."

AT THE GATE

Celia's in a black dress with a striped, artsy scarf looped around her. She tucks her hands into her pockets and leans into the wind, walking away from the car her parents are getting in. Walking toward us.

"Hey," she says.

Janna wraps her arms around Celia. "Hey."

Patrick is next. Simon slaps her five. Matt leans on the stone fence post and nods her way.

I don't know what my response should be, but there's the we-both-lost-a-sister thing in play. Feeling awkward, I open my arms and she steps toward me. She's short and feels more delicate in my arms than I expected. Any words would probably be the wrong words, so I leave it at that.

"Friendly's?" Simon says, as if it's a foregone conclusion.

We end up in a nearby diner, ordering milkshakes, French fries, clam strips, and chicken fingers. It's gonna be a whole heckuva lot of food, but we're equal to the task.

CAN YOU NOT?

"That was fun," I admit. "Simon's such a trip." He spent most of lunch regaling us with ridiculous stories.

"Yeah," Matt agrees. "We have a good time."

Now we're back at Matt's house, just the two of us, in the basement. He immediately heads for his stash.

"Wait."

"What?"

"Can you . . . not? I need you to give me a ride later."

"Just stay over."

"It's Saturday. If I stay, they'll expect us at church tomorrow."

Matt makes a face. "Right. So . . ."

"I'm not calling my parents to come get me, okay? Things got weird this week." They keep giving me a hard time about my refusal to do anything but sleep and see Matt.

He shrugs and tucks the bottle back into its hiding spot. "Okay, well, let's go out and do something, then."

And that's how we end up playing three rounds of laser tag in the midafternoon.

WORLDS COLLIDE

We could laser tag forever, in theory, but neither of us is made of money. Matt more so than me, of course, but even he has an allowance to manage.

"There's a basketball game this afternoon," Matt says. "Want to see if we can catch it?"

"Sure." I'm in the dizzy place, high on us. It's some kind of drug, bumping shoulders in the dark and Matt's breath on my cheek as we scurry to complete our mission. Matt smiles at me and I'd agree to anything.

He holds my hand in the car and I might melt from the calm reassurance of it. If I can stay in this place, the spinning reckless, caught-up-in-you place, I don't have to think or worry. I barely have to breathe. Maybe I will never be moved.

The calm ends as we walk into the gymnasium, join the screaming, cheering crowd in the bleachers.

Why are we here? My brain finally checks me. This is what I don't want, to be seen together. What was I thinking? At least in a movie theater, it's dark. Here, fluorescent lights might as well be pointing a giant arrow at us.

The faces around us are all pointed at the game. No one seems to notice or care as we climb the bleachers, looking for an empty spot to perch. *Maybe it's not so bad*, I try to tell my racing heart. *Maybe it's fine*.

The chaos is not what I crave, though it's consuming in its own way. But my hand is cool and empty and the swirling in my heart slows to a waltz. Here, Matt can't touch me. Here, I'm on my own.

HALFTIME

We stare at the cheerleaders, doing their booty-shaking dance. It's strange, for the first time in my life, to be sitting beside someone who knows what I'm looking at is not the flounce of Janna's flaring skirt, but Adam's rippling arms and chest as he raises her overhead. *He's* looking up her skirt, exposing a column of muscled throat and shoulders like boulders. He wears stretchy leotard pants that leave little to the imagination.

"I was never into team sports," I admit. As a player, I mean. But athletes have great bodies and I'm content to watch them move and bounce. When I used to come with Alex, he would always want to talk about the game. Matt and I sit in near silence, watching.

"That's because you're honest," he answers. Our team runs back onto the court, and we rise, waving our arms along with the cheering crowd.

"What?" I don't get it.

The echoey bounce of the basketball resumes. The squeak of sneakers.

"Being on a team makes people feel like they're in it together," Matt says. "But really everyone is alone."

CONFLICT WITH ALEX

Alex catches me out in the hall, on my way back from the bathroom.

"Hey, Kermit, what gives?" He sounds piqued.

"Huh?"

Alex crosses his arms. "You won't come to the game with me, but you'll come with him?"

Oh. Right. Riiiiight. Shit. "I wasn't planning to come. It just happened."

"You accidentally happened to swing by your least favorite sporting event?"

"Something like that," I mumble. It's the truth.

"Okay," Alex says. "Whatever. Do what you want."

I've hurt his feelings. Not on purpose. Not my fault. Things happen. Why is he on my case?

"You didn't have to lie about it."

That comes out of left field. "How did I lie?"

"You said you didn't want to be at school when you don't have to be."

"I don't." The spiral of how we got here is suddenly clear.

"Yet here you are. Without so much as a text or a hello. With Matt Rincorn, of all people?"

Of all people? I push past the part of my heart that's now offended. "His mom died, okay? He gets things."

"Things I don't get."

I don't want to say it, but . . . yeah. "Look, it's not about us. It's just something that's helping me."

"It's a little about us when you blow me off to hang out with him." Alex crosses his arms.

"It's not like basketball games are our thing or anything. Anyway, you look pretty cozy with Cindy over there. What do you need a third wheel for?"

"That's what this is about? You don't like me being with Cindy?"

"I didn't mean it like that."

"Sounded like it."

My hands cover my face. I scream silently into them. "No, just . . . stop, okay?"

"Mmkay, well, you have fun with your new BFF," Alex says.

"Come on, man."

He stalks off past the concession stand, disappearing behind the line and through the double doors into the gym.

CIRCULAR ARGUMENTS

Yesterday was a lot. Between the Celia stuff and the Alex stuff and generally coming down off the high of me and Matt. My bed is comfortable, my limbs weighty, my stomach a leaden mass, my brain happy to escape into oblivion again and again. To open my eyes is to close them again. Getting up just isn't an option.

I wonder if this is what it's like to feel hungover.

"Up and at 'em," Dad says.

"Not gonna happen," I mutter.

"Oh, yes, sir. We leave in half an hour."

There's nothing to say that can't be said by pulling the blanket over my head.

"Kermit, please," Dad says. "I don't want to do this every week."

"Then there's a simple solution, Dad." Leave me the fuck alone.

He sighs. "You and your mother." The words are so soft I might have misheard him. But it intrigues me enough to pull down the covers. What about Mom?

Dad's standing in the doorway in his khakis, shirt, and loosened tie. "It's advent."

"I'll go on Christmas," I mumble, not sure if that's true. Better to kick the can down the road than cut myself open on it now.

"In this house we have certain obligations," he intones.

"I'm not four. What are you gonna do, drag me kicking and screaming into the sanctuary?"

"Maybe," Dad snaps.

"Hell of a way to make an entrance." I land hard on *hell*.

Dad pounds his fist lightly on the doorframe. Over and over and over, like he's trying to hammer something home, and then his face cracks. He starts crying. "I can't do this," he says. "I don't have the energy,"

"Everyone misses you," Mom tries, rolling up behind Dad, wrapped in her bathrobe. She puts an arm around his waist and rests her cheek on his shoulder. Her hair is mussed and she's been crying, too. We're quite a trio.

"Don't you guys ever want to take a week off?"

"That's not what faith is," Dad manages to say. "It's showing up every week." He clings to the doorframe with the hand that was pounding. *Just let go*, I think. *Float into the atmosphere, where you'll suffocate and die. Like the rest of us.*

Mom says, "I know Pastor Carle would be happy to talk to you about what you're feeling."

What I'm *feeling*? Please.

I don't want to feel. I don't have to feel. I'm like Teflon, untouchable.

"You're not going to change my mind. You're just going to be late." The pillow conforms to my head the way it's been practicing for years. Comforter overhead, and it's a cocoon, as best I can make one.

There's no sound. No further discussion. They're standing

there staring at me, out of sight, for so long it's confusing. I flip over to offer one final retort, but it dies on my tongue.

They've gone.

How long ago? No telling. I didn't hear it.

SUNDAY NIGHT FOOTBALL

Dad knocks on my door. He's wearing his Colts jersey. They're playing the Pats tonight, under the lights of Lucas Oil Stadium. We've been looking forward to this matchup all season.

"Game's on. It would mean a lot to me if you came down and watched with me," Dad says. His reasonable tone is infuriating. "Mom made nachos, Kermit style."

"Kermit style" simply means a gigantic half-sheet pan full of delicious goddamn nachos. I throw off my comforter.

"Fine. But I'm in it for the nachos."

"Duh. Me too," Dad says, rubbing my head as I pass.

In the den, we sit side by side on the loveseat with the sheet pan across our laps. The seat has recliner features, so we pop up the legs and stretch out.

Mom comes in with our Sprites in two big Colts tumblers. She laughs at the sight of us, under the pink blanket, with the napkins tucked into our chins.

"This is not our manliest look," I say when she leaves.

"We are not the manliest of men," Dad says. "Thank goodness."

Sometimes I do that. Float a test balloon, to see how he responds. His track record is pretty good. Dad believes in a softer side of masculinity, a kind where it's okay for a dad and son to snuggle on a loveseat, a kind that means where we are now is about the closest either of us will ever get to an end zone.

We cheers with our Sprites. I don't know where the line is, why it's okay to wear pink and cry tears but not okay to have these other feelings. Why he's comfortable sitting here like this and at the same time I've heard him use words like *unnatural*, *effeminate*, and *queer* in ways that don't feel complimentary.

"Are you ready for some football?" sings a pretty woman in cheerleading garb.

"We are," Dad and I say in unison.

THICK AND THIN

Alex is waiting by my locker, first thing Monday morning. I don't have the energy for this.

"Hey," he says.

"Hey." I go about my business because I can't muster the strength to start anything further.

"I'm sorry," he says. "I shouldn't have been so hard on you."

My gay little mind hears "hard on" and wants to giggle. "Don't worry about it."

"I know it's a rough time for you, and I feel bad about all of what I said."

"Really, it's fine."

"I want to be there for you. Whatever you need." He pauses. "I miss you."

"I'm right here."

But we both know that's not really true.

MAKING UP WITH ALEX

After school he's back. "Do you want to go to Rallyburger on Friday?" The question mark shimmers with the ghost of what he doesn't say: *like we used to*. It used to be an every week thing. It used to be fun.

All I want on the weekends now is Matt. Our quiet, our fun, our ability to pretend we're on an island.

"I'm sorry," I tell Alex, and I actually mean it. If I could turn back time, I'd love nothing more. But time marches on.

"You don't ever want to hang out anymore," Alex says. His voice is soft and sad, not angry. "It's like the old you died with your sister. I hate it."

I hate it, too.

"We're still best friends," I tell him.

"Are we?"

"Of course. Anyway, you've got Cindy now."

"Yeah." He shuffles his feet. "It's not like I don't have other friends. But I miss you."

Damn. He's got me slipping close to the edge of the man-feels. We're going to end up hugging in the hallway like the massive nerds we are.

"I met someone, too," I blurt out. "I've been spending time with . . . them."

"Really? You're, like, dating someone?"

"I didn't tell you because . . . well, I didn't tell anyone."

"Who is it?"

"I can't tell you."

"It's Matt Rincorn, isn't it?"

I must be blushing. Alex nods knowingly.

"I thought there was something weird there. Not weird, just . . . weird. I sensed it."

I'm dismayed. "Is it really obvious? No one's supposed to know."

Alex shrugs. "I know you. You've had a thing for him forever."

"You knew?"

"Didn't you know I had a thing for Cindy all along?"

Fair point. "Sure."

Alex slugs my arm. "You can probably chill out about it being a secret. People are cool with Matt. They'll be cool with you, too."

If only it was that easy.

GUYS, INTERRUPTED

It's easier to say yes to Alex, now that he knows the truth. When I tell him I changed my mind about Friday, he lights up.

"But, would it be cool if we didn't go to Rallyburger? I'm not really up for being in public around a lot of people from school." School itself is about all I can take these days.

"Sure," Alex says. "We can order pizza."

We settle in with pizza and snacks, diving into a video game marathon that throws us back to middle school. The familiar is comforting and it strikes me how much I'd have been missing this if my brain wasn't soup most of the time.

It's pretty late, almost ten, when Alex's phone starts lighting up.

"Cindy." He smiles. "She's drunk texting me from Steve's party."

"Cute."

His thumbs work the phone. "This girl, man. Get a couple of drinks in her and anything can happen."

"Sounds like she keeps you on your toes." *I know the feeling.*

"Definitely." He grins, then stops. "Shit."

"What?"

Alex bites his lip. "Um. So . . . you know how you 'coincidentally ended up going' to the game with Matt? And I got mad?"

"We don't have to rehash—"

"No, no," he says. "But now I, uh, totally get how that could happen." He's being super vague.

I turn my palm up. "Meaning?"

"Don't be mad." Alex looks chagrined, like he's about to ask for my kidney or something.

"What?"

"Cindy's DD just bailed on Steve's party. She wants to know if I can come get her on the way to dropping you off."

Among my shittier best friend moves of late: my total failure to celebrate with Alex over getting his driver's license. Fuck. I'm awful. I assumed his mom would be driving me home later.

"Oh. You told her yeah, right?"

"Yeah. And I know I promised you a quiet night, but . . ." He grimaces.

"But her getting ditched isn't cool and you want to go there now and make sure she's okay."

Alex sighs, relieved. "Yeah."

I shrug. "So let's go."

PUBLIC EXERCISE IN LOSERDOM (THE SECOND)

"I'm really sorry, Kerm," Alex says. We're walking up the drive toward the chaos that is Steve's party.

"Don't worry." I nudge his shoulder. "It's a small price to pay for having such a good guy as my best friend." *And maybe Matt is here.* The thought zings in the back of my mind.

Matt and Kermit sitting in a tree, sings Sheila. *K-I-S-S-I-N-G.*

"Well, I appreciate it. I'll just be a minute." Alex goes looking for Cindy.

"Take your time," I call after him. "We're here now."

Matt wasn't on the porch swing. He isn't in the foyer. He isn't in the kitchen, either, but I nod hello to a tipsy-looking Janna, who nods back. She stretches out an arm toward me, motioning me closer. She's standing with two other junior girls.

"Kerm," she says, "Fancy meeting you here."

"You good?" I ask her, unsure if it's a breach of club rules. We don't really run in the same circles normally. But the Venn diagram of our social lives seems to have some overlap tonight.

"Yeah, good," she says. "It's a good night. You just getting here?"

"Yeah." It's unclear how much is okay to say in front of her other friends, so I smile awkwardly.

"We've been dancing up a storm," Janna says. "You just missed a long set."

"Maybe it'll come around again," I say. Not like I'd be caught dead dancing at a party.

"If you're looking for Matt, maybe try that way," she adds, tilting her head toward the dining room. "And tread lightly."

Not sure what that means. "Thanks. Have fun." I touch her arm, then circle through the dining room into the living room.

"Kermit Sanders," Matt calls. "Wherever you go, there you are."

PUBLIC EXERCISE IN LOSERDOM (CONTINUED)

"I thought you weren't coming tonight." Matt wobbles toward me, unsteady on his feet. He trips across the rug and slams his shoulder into the wall. He leans there and crosses one leg over the other, like he meant to do that. "Dude, you showed up."

"Alex talked me into it." No need to get into the details that brought us here.

"Hey, great. Good to see you, man." His drunkenness makes the casual tone sound exactly as forced as it is.

"Yeah, you too."

Matt runs a hand through his hair and smiles at me. His floppiness is weirdly sexy. I remember Alex saying, "get a couple drinks in Cindy and anything might happen." It occurs to me to push Matt back against the wall and kiss him, right here in front of everyone. But he wouldn't stop me from doing that, even sober. I'm the one holding us back from it, always.

Anyway, he pushes himself against the wall, leaning his whole back on it and closing his eyes.

"Looks like someone's had a pretty good time tonight."

He opens one eye. "Hell no. This party's a total snooze. I was about to peace out."

Peace out or pass out, I wonder.

"Come across the street with me," Matt whispers. "My dad's not home."

"I can't leave. I'm here with Alex."

"Alex has Cindy in the front hall closet. I'm thinking you can probably step away for a minute."

PRIVATE EXERCISE IN LOSERDOM (ONGOING)

"**Dad keeps much** better liquor than that shit Steve serves."

"Hmm?" I'm focusing on my two open text threads. I tell Alex I'm having Mom pick me up at Rallyburger so he and Cindy can have the night and enjoy their midnight curfew.

Stay and have fun, I write now. I'm tired anyway. We can do something tomorrow.

I tell Mom I'm staying the night at Alex's house, which brings up a little emotional fuss, but nothing that can't be talked down with: *Chill, Mom. I love you.*

Now I tuck the phone away. Matt's rummaging around his dad's liquor cabinet. "Won't he notice if you take stuff?"

"Never has before."

"I also think maybe you've had enough."

He's struggling to get the cap off the bottle of brown liquor he's chosen.

I put my hand on his back. "You want a snack? I could eat."

"Open this," he says, thrusting the bottle at me.

I take it. "Let's get a snack."

We go into the kitchen. I don't know a lot about what to do

with a very drunk person, but TV suggests things like coffee, food, and water are a better bet than more booze.

"Where's your dad?" The office where he's been stationed every time I've been over is dark.

"I don't know," he says. "Probably off with *her*."

Ah. "Girlfriend?"

"Dunno. I never meet them."

"Them? So it's like that?"

"I don't fucking know," he says. "I don't wanna talk . . . it." He leans over the counter island, stretching his arms in front of him. "Fuck."

The closet is a treasure trove of snack foods. Corn chips sound good. A couple bags of those plus a package of M&M's feels about right.

"Here, what about this?"

"Yeah." Matt snatches a chip bag and lurches toward the living room. I fill up two glasses of water and follow.

Matt stands at the edge of the rug, tears the chip bag open, and pours the pieces all over the leather couch. "If he tries to bring that bitch in here, she'll think we live like rodents and run away."

"I thought you were okay with him dating." Something he said in passing once made me think this.

"I don't care if he dates. I care if he brings them home."

"Does he usually?"

"I don't fucking know," he says. "He's really fucking discreet. But I can smell their perfume. In the mornings. From somewhere." He waves his hand around. "On him. Or in here. I don't fucking know." He throws the empty foil bag at the matching armchair.

"How does it look?" he asks, stroking his chin. "Crappy enough?"

"I'd say so." It's impossible to look away from him. He radiates anger and pain, with a baldness that I've never seen in anyone. There's some kind of power in it. It draws me to him, but at the same time, I can't overlook the state he's in.

"I think, maybe, it's time to go to bed," I suggest.

He lurches toward me. "You wanna go to bed with me?"

"I meant—"

It's easier than it should be to kiss him like this. He's buttersoft and melting against me. Corn chips crackle underneath my back. Matt's fingers tease my hairline as his palms slide along the sides of my face.

Matt slides down and kisses my throat. "I want us to do it," he whispers.

"We can't do it," I whisper.

"I have all the stuff," he says. "We could do it."

I shake my head and I'm breathless. "No. Just like usual." We can kiss until we come and I'll borrow his boxers. It's worked really well up to this point.

"You know you want to," he pants.

I do want to. Sort of. But I can't. *We* can't. "Not now, though."

"Don't be a chickenshit."

"Don't be a bully."

"Chickenshit."

I scramble out from under him, landing on my ass on the rug. "Bully."

Matt flops face-first onto the couch. Laughing. "Come back, silly." He pushes himself up, about half successfully. "I'm just messing with you."

I crawl toward the fireplace. "Maybe I'd want to if you weren't so drunk."

"Naw," he says. "Maybe if you weren't so scared."

"You're mean when you're drunk."

"Don't say that." Matt pushes himself up. "Never say that!" And suddenly he's crying.

I don't know what to do.

Matt rolls on the couch cushions, crunching corn chips and weeping. I crawl toward him.

"Hey."

He leans against me, trembling. His whole face waters onto my shirtsleeves. I hold him in my arms, across my lap, and we shake with the force of his tears.

Then he's finally still for a moment, like maybe he's cried himself to sleep.

Then he moans. "Uh-oh." A retching sound arises in his throat.

Never have I moved so fast. I grab the wastebasket that's near the couch and thrust it under his face.

Now we're in territory I understand. I put one hand under his shoulder and use the other to steady the wastebasket. Luckily it's lined with a plastic bag. I hold my breath so the smell doesn't send me down the rabbit hole right after him.

SECRETS

When it's over, I leave Matt prone on the couch, with his cheek at the edge of the cushion, while I get a cool towel from the kitchen. I wipe his mouth and face and hand, the way my parents always did when one of us was sick. I help him sit up, so he can drink a little water and rinse out the bad taste. He doesn't seem to care that much.

"Why are you helping me?" he mutters. "Just leave me, it's fine."

I laugh. "Um, I beg to differ. This is not your finest hour."

"Like you're so perfect?"

"That's beside the point."

"Maybe you are," he says. "Maybe you know all the secrets."

"I don't know your secrets," I say. "Are you going to tell me?"

"I'll tell you anything," he says. "If you promise not to leave."

I couldn't if I wanted to. There's no chance I'm calling my parents or Alex in the middle of the night and getting caught in a lie. So where would I go? And the truth is, I don't want to go. Matt's curled softly in my arms and for a change it seems like he needs me, the way I need him.

"Anything? Then tell me what you think about me, for real," I whisper.

"I think you're hot," he says, reaching for me.

"Come on." I laugh. "Really? I'm pretty sure anyone looking at us would agree that you're the hot one."

"You're so smart."

That one, I'll take. "Thanks."

"Smart to never tell. Shhh. Never tell. Be out."

My forehead wrinkles. "What are you talking about?"

"Never tell," he says. "We can be shhhh." He's not making sense.

"It's okay." I stroke his shoulder. "Never mind."

"No," he says. "You have to trust me. I know and I don't want you to find out."

"Find out?"

"So you'll never know the truth."

"What's the truth?"

"That they'll never accept us."

It stings. A heat sizzles across my heart. "Who? My parents?"

"No, the whole world."

TOO MUCH

Matt throws up again, rolling out of my arms and onto the floor in the process. I wipe him off, prop his back against the couch, and put a pillow under his head when he passes out. The couch is still a mess of corn chip crumbs and I'm pretty sure a sober Matt would disapprove, so I sweep up all signs of his tantrum, brushing the last crumbs under the couch. I hold my breath as I clear out the trash bag, then rummage in the kitchen for a new liner for the wastebasket.

The second bag of corn chips is still intact, but not for long. Busting into it takes the edge off my nerves for a minute. What I feel echoes what Matt said after we went to church that time. *Tonight was too much.*

Each corn chip feels like it weighs fifty pounds, or maybe it's my arm that's heavy, from the weight of everything going on. It's strange, being in this place that has become so familiar and always felt so safe, and feeling suddenly completely alone.

Matt's dad is still not home; it's one in the morning. Surely he'll be back soon. For a time, my only thoughts are what to say if Mr. Rincorn walks in and finds me snacking in his kitchen alone in the single digits. 'Cause that's not weird.

Luckily it's not a problem. He doesn't come in. I eat the entire bag of chips and drink my glass of water. Matt seems okay—for certain values of okay—so there's not much else to do but lie down on the couch above him and try to get some sleep.

HEART OF THE NIGHT

My eyes open, struggling to focus. Matt's nudging me. The wall clock says 4:00 A.M.

"Hey." He kneels beside the couch, his face close to mine.

"Hey." I roll toward him.

"What are you doing here?"

"Um, helping you?"

"Oh."

"Why? You don't remember?"

He shakes his head. "I'm pretty messed up," he says, gazing blankly at me. "I have no idea what the fuck is going on."

"It's the middle of the night," I say. "Just lie back down and sleep some more."

"We should go to my room," he says, grabbing my hand as if to lead the way. But then he just kneels there, blinking at me.

"Okay." I push off the couch, tugging him up by the hand. "Can you walk now?"

"Good as the day I was born," he says, which makes no sense, but neither of us laughs.

I make him drink some of the water in the glass, and then we go upstairs. He holds my hand the whole way. Can't help the fleeting thought that this is what it might be like to walk down the halls of our school together, hand in hand.

In his room, I start looking for the sleeping bags we used before.

"Fuck that," Matt says, pushing off his jeans and crawling into the bed. He pats the spot next to him. "Come in here."

A heartbeat of hesitation later, my jeans fall beside his on the floor. It's not too hard to act chill, but it still feels momentous, my first time sharing an actual bed with a guy. We slide under the sheets, side by side. Matt rolls to face me, sliding his hand across my stomach and tugging me closer. His warm knees embrace my bare thigh and he rests his forehead on my shoulder.

"You feel good," he murmurs. "I always want it to be like this. You and me." He snuggles against me and I can't help wondering if he's still drunk.

The warmth where he's touching me is stirring. I rest my cheek against the top of his head.

"Why are you here?" he murmurs. "Why don't you hate me like everyone else?"

"What? You're so popular. Everyone loves you."

"Nah," he says. "It's an act. None of it is real." *They'll never accept us.* Matt's words float back to me with a chill.

My hand touches his arm, resting across me. My thumb smooths his little arm hairs into place. "So what is real?"

"You."

A tiny trill strikes the core of me. "Yeah?"

"The club. I live for that shit, man."

"Sometimes you just need someone there with you?" That's

what he said to me once, about Janna, but maybe he was talking about himself. Maybe he was talking about all of us.

"Janna and I started it two years ago. Her accident happened less than a month before my mom took the last turn, you know, the moment when we knew it was going to happen, and after that point, it was over like that." He brushes his fingers together, in a silent snap, against my hip. "She was just gone. There was all this sudden attention and things got weird and Janna and I just kind of found each other in the middle of it. We started dating—this was before I was out—but even back then it was always this sort of fake-dating where we would mostly use each other as an excuse not to get together with other people. Then we would hang out and not talk about stuff, and it was so great. Because she got it, right?"

"Sure."

"And so she was the first person I told, other than my mom, and when I came out she was there for me through everything. She's like my best friend, even though we don't act like it. That's the whole point. And why the club is secret, because you have to keep living your life even when you feel like crap inside."

"Yeah." This, I understand.

He's crying again. The dampness spreads through my shirt at the shoulder.

"Hey." I shift so I can put my arm around him. "It's okay."

He rolls toward me, landing half on top, half alongside. My body aches with pleasure. "If we make out, it will be."

He's forgotten what he said downstairs. The way he pushed and the way he hurt me. Maybe I should forget, too.

"I just want to feel good. Don't you?"

"Sure."

His mouth is near mine and yeah, of course, I want this. Gentle and intimate, with our hearts open in the quiet and the dark. This is more like how it should be.

There are tear tracks on his cheeks and it's unbearably sexy. With my thumb I wipe one side away.

"Shit." Matt runs a hand through his hair, then wipes his other cheek himself. "Sorry . . . I didn't mean to unload it all like that. Let's pretend I didn't."

"It's okay."

"You must think I'm a total freak."

Um, actually I think you're the god of everything. "No, I'm with you."

"Yeah?"

"Yeah." I tip my mouth upward. *Completely and totally with you.*

NO SEX

The less-drunk version of Matt respects my boundaries. He puts his hand on my penis for the first time, then guides my hand to his. I don't need anything more than that to feel thrilled, elated, carried to a different plane.

DOWN FOR THE COUNT

Bright sun streams in Matt's bedroom window, striking me in the eye. It's too early. Normally he remembers to close the curtains at night, so this doesn't happen. I roll toward Matt, putting my back to the sun, but the warmth spreads over my neck. It's morning. No hiding from it. The magic of the dark has been stolen, the spell of our whispered thoughts broken. What had felt perfect now feels cheapened, flawed, exposed. My body itself radiates a shameful heat that rivals the dawn.

I don't regret what happened. Not at all. That's the problem. I'm slipping, fast and hard. Sleeping beside Matt, letting him touch me. Wanting him.

Kermit: zero. Impure thoughts: one million.

Someday soon there will be no turning back. I'll be lost to my sins forever. I can feel it. And I don't know what to do.

Matt's sound asleep still. He doesn't notice me slip out of the bedroom.

ABANDONED

Matt's still asleep. I sit on the living room floor, staring at the blank television. I could probably watch something. Or pull a book off the shelf, but instead I'm frozen on the carpet, feeling like a complete loser.

I can't call Mom or Dad or be caught in a lie, plus it's too early. *Fruit of the poisonous tree*, Sheila says. *Serves you right.*

So I text Alex to see if he wants to meet up for lunch later. At least then I'd have a plan. A place to be other than here, eventually.

Can't, he writes. *I have to go to a birthday party with Cindy that I forgot about. But I have all day tomorrow free.*

At least he sees now. Things can happen. It doesn't mean you don't care.

Okay, sounds good.

So it's just me, then. Sitting here on someone else's floor.

Alone.

RETRIEVAL

Rallyburger opens at eleven on Saturdays. They don't do breakfast. I'm on the sidewalk at 10:55, waiting.

I text Dad to pick me up here at eleven thirty, saying Alex has to be somewhere, but we're going to eat first. It's a realistic time and a believable reason to need a ride.

It's both my parents who arrive to get me, together, after a bit of Christmas shopping, I gather, from the mounds of store bags in the hatchback.

They don't ask questions, which is a relief, since I have no answers.

APOLOGY

Matt's on my doorstep in the midafternoon, hat in hand, meta-phorically. He wears a ski cap and a fleece vest, shifting his feet like he's shy. My parents are out, still shopping, so I invite him in because I don't feel like getting in the car and trying to go somewhere.

We stand in the living room, the space reserved for guests we don't know that well or who drop by unexpectedly.

"Look, I'm really sorry about last night."

"Okay." Maybe I should have more to say, but nothing comes to mind.

"I've been trying not to get wasted in front of you," he says, moving closer. "I know it bothers you. I didn't know you were coming to the party."

"Is that what you're like?" I ask. "When we're not together?"

Matt tugs at my belt loops. "I like to party. You know that."

"It didn't look like much fun," I admit. "After a certain point."

He looks away. "Yeah, I had a little too much. I know that. But you know it's not always like that."

"I know." The back of my mind whispers a warning I ignore. Because he's here now, and close to me, and promising deli-cious distraction.

"Can you forgive me?" He makes a sweet puppy-dog face. I roll my eyes. Maybe it shouldn't be that easy, but it is. I can't stay mad at him. It's not even that I was mad to begin with, exactly, but to name the feeling would take more energy than I have.

And to tell the truth, Matt's the only person I can really count on these days. I need him.

HEAVY

Matt takes me back to the state park, to the cliffside. We hike, we shout into the void of the air, we laugh, we huddle together in the chill winter air and sip cocoa from the thermoses Matt prepared. We're goofy.

For the first time, being here, what surrounds us feels like an absence more than a fullness. We are breathless and elevated, but also disconnected, somehow, from the landscape. From each other.

I don't miss ultra-drunk Matt, but I want more of the closeness we had last night, with him in my arms whispering to me about his heart. At the same time I want to fly free, like we do sometimes, to be epic and beautiful and pretend everything is perfect.

"You told me a little about your mom, and about starting the club with Janna."

"I did?" he says.

It's weird that he doesn't remember. It's like that night doesn't even exist for anyone but me, like one of my dreams. Maybe it was all in my head.

"I'd like to know more about her."

"I don't like to talk about it," he says, which doesn't feel true to me. Sometimes, in the night, he whispers things. But in retrospect, I guess, it's only when he's been drinking. Thinking on that casts all our hammock nights in a different light, even the times when he seemed fine all along.

"You also said no one would ever accept us."

"I don't feel accepted," he says.

"I don't understand." The image of him, always surrounded by adoring crowds, is all I can picture.

"I don't want you to understand," he says. "I want to protect you."

"You don't have to protect me."

"Yeah," he says. "You're already so sad. I don't want you to have to deal with anything more. Look at those birds." He points. "What kind do you think they are? Their ancestors were dinosaurs, you know."

"Then they must be pterodactyls," I answer, which leads to a long riff on our favorite dinosaurs.

"We were talking for a minute," I say, trying to bring it back to that tender place we touched briefly.

"No," he says. "From now on today we only talk about things that fly. Hot-air balloons. Bats. Flying squirrels."

"Airplanes?"

"Too obvious."

"Starships?"

"Better."

"But less real."

"Says who? You're the *Star Trek* fan among us."

I enjoy who we are when we're like this, goofy and free and shooting the shit. Truly. And yet, the craving in my bones hasn't gone away. "Tell me something real."

"Kermit, you're bringing us down," Matt answers. "You tell me something outlandish."

The sky, the trees, the clouds, the air, the rocks, the grass, the fog of our breath. So many things around us scream their truth. How can we be embedded in the midst of nature and still somehow be floating?

"I don't know if what we have is real if you have to be drunk to talk about stuff."

"I only said that stuff *because* I was drunk," he says. "That doesn't make it real. There's a difference."

"So tell me something real."

Matt looks out over the treetops. "I don't want to get heavy right now," he says. "I want to get out of my head, don't you?"

"Sure."

He pulls the tarp out of his backpack. "Then let's be epic," he says. "Let's be beautiful."

We cliff jump for the better part of an hour. And somewhere between the sky and the ground, I forget to care about anything.

I, SOCELES

My parents sit across from me, both on the same side of the table, facing me. When we used to have family meetings, we would sit in our regular dinnertime places. Me across from Dad and Sheila across from Mom. Now we're a triangle, not a square. And not an equilateral triangle, an isoceles. The side between the two of them is short. The sides between each of them and me are long.

"We're a little concerned," Dad says. "You seem . . . you're not yourself. You've become very withdrawn."

I don't know what to say to that. How am I supposed to be myself under the circumstances? Who even is that anymore? Whole parts of me have been scooped away. I'm hollow, like a decorative melon.

"You don't seem to be showing the signs of grief that we've been expecting."

This, from the guy who complains about my sleep patterns. I roll my eyes. "Read about it in a book, there, did ya?"

Dad looks slightly embarrassed. "Well . . ."

"Honey," Mom interjects, patting Dad's arm. He falls quiet, biting his lip. "We just wanted to talk to you for a minute. We want to know how you're doing."

My life has shattered into a million pieces, like Sheila's windshield. And probably her face. *Don't forget my face*, she whispers. My chest clenches.

"I'm doing okay."

"You know you can talk to us," Dad says. "About whatever you're feeling."

"I'm not feeling anything."

Dad frowns. "Kerm, that's not true."

Gee, thanks, Captain Obvious. "I don't want to talk about what I'm feeling."

"You've been so strong," Mom says. "But you don't need to do that with us."

It surprises me when she says that. Strong? Me? "What is the point of this? Do you want me to cry in front of you or something?"

Mom reaches for my hand. "Do you cry when you're alone?"

"That wasn't what I was saying."

"Do you?" Her voice taps at a dark piece of my shame.

"Not everybody cries about stuff, Mom."

I let her stroke the back of my hand even though it is maddening to be touched in this soft way.

"You've always been a sensitive boy," Mom says. Sheila giggles. *He's a gay boy, Mom. Go figure.* "You two were so close. We just—we expected to see this affecting you more."

"This?" Dad nudges.

Mom closes her eyes. "Sheila's death. We expected to see Sheila's death affecting you more."

Good job, Mom. Way to really say it. Mom is working on keeping the loss concrete in her language. I know because I live here.

They think I don't know all these things about them, but I do. So why is it that they don't know so many things about me?

"Let me get this straight. You're concerned about how well I'm doing?"

"You don't have to be doing well, sweetie," Mom says. "I—" Her voice cracks. She clutches my hand. "I am not doing well."

"Not exactly a news flash. We all know that," I mutter.

"Kerm," Dad scolds, as Mom starts bawling in earnest. "Apologize to your mother."

"For what?" I throw my hands out. "For agreeing with her?"

"For your tone of voice."

We've got tone, Sheila says, imitating the husky voice of a missile launch commander. *Missiles locked. Fire when ready.*

I push away from the table. "Maybe that's just how I'm doing."

I storm away and act like I'm going upstairs, but really I just pound my feet on the first step and sit down. I want to hear what they're going to say about me after I'm gone.

"Well, you got your answer," Dad says.

Mom sobs. The sound is muffled, I assume because she's pressing her face into the plastic-laminated tabletop.

"I'd be more worried if he'd been polite and obedient. Wouldn't you?"

Mom sobs. I imagine Dad rubbing her back with one hand, although, come to think of it, he didn't touch her at all when she started crying before.

As if to prove this thought, Dad's chair scrapes back. Empty dinner plates clatter. Water runs. And runs. And runs.

I lean against the stair railing, listening to Mom cry while Dad washes the dishes. Even though they make it seem like they're in it together, maybe sadness is actually the kind of thing everyone handles by themselves. Strangely, knowing that makes me feel a little less alone.

WEIGHTLESS

At the start of Christmas break, Matt takes me winter camping. This is off-the-charts high on the list of things I never thought I'd do. We bustle around in our mittens setting up the tent and stacking wood in the firepit. It's not polar-vortex cold or anything, but it's in the high forties and bound to get cooler overnight.

"How did you learn to do all of this?" I ask as he whips an extra tarp over the tent we just pitched.

"We used to go camping all the time," he says.

It seems strange to me. My parents' idea of vacation is a Holiday Inn with a pool, somewhere in driving distance.

"It's hard to picture your dad camping."

"He only came sometimes."

So this was a Matt and his mom thing. I'm learning to read between the lines to hear what he doesn't say. He's stacked the firewood carefully in a square in the firepit.

"Should we light it?" I ask.

"When we get back." He kisses me, out in the open, under the trees.

"Where are we going?"

"Hiking." Matt opens the thermoses and inspects them. "This one's yours."

"What did you put in yours?" I ask.

"A little something extra," he says.

The eternal tug-of-war tightens my gut. "I thought you were cutting back."

"I am. But I have to stay warm, so I can keep you warm."

The logic works for me, when his face is so close to mine.

TIPSY

Our legs dangle over the separate world of plants and bugs and earth and birds below us. It looks to me less like nothingness, and more like otherness. Down-belowness. A mystery, not a void.

We're bundled up, sipping our hot cocoa. The stillness is something powerful. We link our arms because we can't hold hands in these mittens. I love this place because Matt brings me here, but I doubt I'll ever love it the way he does.

"You wanted to know more about my mom?" he says. "She's the one who showed me this place." Matt's hot cocoa–plus kicks in and the switch flips.

"I figured. She sounds really cool."

"I never thought of it that way, but yeah. I see it now." He sips his cocoa and the next breath he releases fogs extra hard from the warmth.

"My mom knew I was gay," he says. "She just said 'I know, honey. I love you.'"

"You're lucky. I could never tell my mom about us."

"Well, she was dying and all. It wasn't in her interest to get upset about it."

"Stop," I say. "You don't really think of it like that, right?"

He shrugs. Throws a pebble into the abyss and watches it fall. "She stopped caring about real-world things."

"Dying puts things into perspective, or something?"

"My mom used to say, 'Someday the world will know who you are and they'll love you.' I think that's why I came out, to try to hold on to that piece of her, that promised me things would be okay."

"Even though it's supposed to be not that big a deal in the world right now, there's still no way I can tell my parents," I say. "My sister was going to help me."

He glances at me. "It's cool that she knew."

I nod.

"That's huge, really."

"She's cool about it. At least, she used to be?"

"Used to be?" he echoes.

But I can't tell him all about the dreams, or how real they feel. "She can't be cool now that she's dead, right?"

"I don't know," he says. "At least they both died knowing." He throws another pebble, watches it fall.

I nod. The losses are so very different and yet so much the same. "We'll always have that." I say it more for his benefit than mine, but it's true. It's something to hold on to.

"Can we make out now?" he says.

"Not at the edge."

He cups a hand behind my neck. "Live a little."

The way he kisses is as good as a tumble. There are still rocks beneath my butt, and grass in my clenched fist, but sure enough I am falling.

COME WITH ME

"I wish you'd come with me," he says into the firelight.

"Where?" I've already followed him to the top of the world. It's surprisingly warm here, in his arms by the fire, with snow flurries dusting the air around us. The temperature must've dropped, but I don't feel it.

"One little sip," he says. "So you can relax and be free."

Oh. "Sorry. Peer pressure doesn't really work on me." That much is true. I've never even been tempted before. It's never really been a thing for me at all.

"You're not even a little bit curious?" He sounds amazed, disbelieving.

A part of me is curious as hell, and I'm already on the outs with God, so there's no coherent logic to my resistance.

"I'm happy being here with you."

"If you come with me, we won't be here anymore."

Stay with me, I want to counter. "Then what if we both disappear?"

"Maybe it would be perfect," he says. "Maybe it would be beautiful."

WINTER CAMPING

My parents would never let me go camping alone with a girl, for obvious reasons. It's quiet, and by the wavering light of the campfire, Matt looks almost unbearably sexy. He twines his fingers with mine and we rock back in the low chairs he's brought. They hover inches off the ground, keeping us from the chill earth, with our legs stretched out on either side of the blaze we continue to feed.

"Are we gonna have sex?" I blurt out.

"Do you want to?" he says.

I spied the condoms in Matt's bag and my heart is full of questions. Other parts of me are full and my body shakes, slow tremors pulsing outward from my bones.

"You brought protection."

"It's just good sense," Matt says. "But peer pressure doesn't work on you, remember?"

"Have you ever—?"

"No," Matt says. "Except with you." As far as we know, we are the only two gay guys at our school. We can't be, of course, but it's as far as we know.

"Me?"

He's quiet for a moment. "I feel like we already have had sex, don't you?"

It startles me to my core. "No!"

"Really?" He sounds as surprised as I feel. "That's defining sex pretty narrowly, don't you think? What we do doesn't have to parallel straight people's idea of sex."

"The things we've done don't count." It's important to me that they not count.

"Relax. That's not why I brought you up here," he says, but he leans over and kisses me anyway.

FIRELIGHT

My words must've upset Matt more than he let on. The soft and mellow mood we'd been cultivating is rocked. It's subtle, but discernable. The pot with our cocoa rests in the coals but soon I'm the only one reaching for it. Matt reaches for his special flask, losing the pretense of cocoa altogether.

"What's happening?" I ask gently. "Is it me?"

"Kermit, you're perfect and beautiful," he says. He moves from his own chair, sliding across the cold ground to meet me. When we kiss, it's electric.

He pulls me forward, onto the cushion that's keeping our feet from touching the earth. His thighs press the outside of mine. For a time, the cold means nothing. There is only fire.

TENT

It's not like last time. Matt doesn't get sick, but I do have to help him into the tent. He stares at me with soft eyes, petting my chest as we sit atop the sleeping bag.

"Take your shirt off. Why isn't your shirt off?"

"It's too cold," I tell him, working the laces of his boots. "We have to sleep in our clothes."

"I'll keep you warm."

"Promises, promises."

"I will," he insists. "You can trust me."

I take his face in my hands. "I'm sorry for what I said."

"So you *will* take your shirt off?" He laughs. "Then I win!" He leans into my shoulder, still laughing.

"It all counts, Matt. Everything we've ever done matters to me so much."

"Me too."

Earlier, he opened the two sleeping bags we brought, flattening them out and zipping them together into one large bag for us to share. The sleeping bag surface is slick, and it's all that separates us. His eyes flicker with heat.

We slide inside together, fast and awkward, huddling close.

The pillow is cold but our bodies quickly warm the bag and it's surprisingly cozy. Matt snuggles his back against me and I wrap my arm around him. Little spoon, big spoon.

"When you said 'winter camping' I was pretty skeptical," I admit.

"You hid it well." Matt laughs, meaning the opposite.

"I get it now."

"I'm glad. It's been a long time since I could do this."

"Your mom loved camping, huh?"

"Yeah." He tells me a semi-coherent story about the last time he and his mom came up here, shortly after her diagnosis. "I thought I'd never do it again," he admits. "But it's good, right? That we did it?"

"Yeah." My hand smooths over his. "I hope you remember telling me these things in the morning. I want you to know that I know."

"Maybe I want to forget," he mutters. "Maybe I want to forget my whole fucking life."

"Say more about that," I whisper.

"It's nothing. Or everything. Fuck. Never mind." He pulls his knees up tighter, and I curve mine behind them, to match.

"Don't keep it in. Is it something from home? Something from school?"

He's quiet for a moment. "You saw, didn't you? In the locker room."

"Matt, how did you really get those bruises?" I ask softly.

"You don't understand," he says. "No one knows about you. You have no idea how bad it gets."

"Tell me."

"Sometimes after gym class," he says, "Richie Corner pushes me against my locker and tries to feel my butthole."

"That's messed up." My stomach knots with the ache of it. Having suspicions was one thing but knowing is worse.

"Yeah."

"More than messed up," I amend. "It's maybe, technically, a crime." Locker room ribbing and joshing is a thing that happens, but a cut lip, and bruises, and trying to touch his butt?

Matt is quiet. "You won't tell, will you?"

"Not if you don't want me to."

"The one time I tried to say something, it just got worse after."

I rub his arm. "You're always so cheerful at school. I don't think I could be if that was happening to me." Everyone has stuff going on under the surface, I guess, but Matt's energy is so large and bright in that landscape. It's hard to reconcile.

"Gay means happy," he says. "People have expectations. Too much *Queer Eye* or something."

"You're a real people-pleaser."

"I could definitely make it in Hollywood." His voice goes blurry. "Smile for the camera."

TENSION TAMER

Sunrise in the campground is cold and white. A light layer of snow has fallen, rendering everything beautiful. But the striking white veneer over the dry brown earth is thin. Our boot prints disrupt the snow as we dig for warm coals beneath the remnants of burned-out logs.

"There's always something under the surface," Matt says. "Just have to uncover it."

Soon there's a dry circle of coals on which we light the fresh wood Matt had the forethought to keep in our tent overnight.

Cooking eggs and bacon over the campfire is easier than I would have expected and tastes amazing for the effort. We boil a brick of cocoa and settle on the low chairs to warm ourselves by the rekindled fire.

"How do you feel?" I ask.

Matt grins his goofiest grin and the incongruity is striking. "Never better. You?"

"Yeah, great." There are more things I want to say, to ask, but that smile makes it clear that serious topics won't be welcome in the daylight.

THEN: 'TIS THE SEASON (ONE YEAR AGO)

Christmas music rocks from Sheila's stereo and we dance along, stringing popcorn and cranberries onto a mile-long coil of thread, arguing.

"Is too," Sheila says.

"Is not!" I declare.

"Is too." Sheila sighs. "What are we, four?"

"Easter is the biggest holiday, for Christians."

"Easter is the most *important* holiday," she says. "Christmas is the biggest. Come on, a couple little chocolate baskets, versus all this." She throws her arms out, indicating the red, white, and green explosion around us.

"Semantics," I protest. "Biggest, most important."

"It's two different things," Sheila insists.

"The entire faith is built around the resurrection," I argue. "That's fact."

"Anyway, think about it—if Jesus wasn't born, how could he die on the cross thirty-three years later and save all our sins and give us new life, yadda, yadda."

"Noo," I moan.

"Next year at this time, I'll be away at college," she reminds me. "You won't have me around to set you straight about these things." She winks. "I mean, set you on the right track."

I glance at the doorway, hoping Mom and Dad didn't hear. "Stop it," I whisper. "Don't do that."

"Oh, Kermie. If I don't give you a hard time, who will?" Her grin wins me over, as always.

"It's rarely a value add," I grumble. "Ow." The garland needle pricks me, as if to draw my attention back to the task.

"By the way, I'm wearing my green dress tonight. Will you wear a green tie to match?"

"Only if you admit I'm right," I say, sucking the drop of blood off my finger. "My actual theology beats your gifts versus chocolate theory."

Sheila pauses her stringing and looks at me with half a smile. "Sure, Kerm, you win. You're the better Christian."

NOW: FLURRY

Christmas break comes with various family obligations and church stuff. Most of it I manage to dodge, but thanks to the terms of the tenuous truce with my parents about attendance, I'm stuck at home most of the pre-Christmas week.

Mom's determined to decorate like always. Maybe she's forgotten that it was Sheila who cared. Or maybe it's because of that.

No one knows what to do with her stocking. Putting out only three looks weird and feels wrong. But will it be weirder to have all four laid out for advent, only to have one still empty on Christmas morning? An inordinate amount of my brain space goes toward this problem.

"We could skip it," I say to Mom, in case it hasn't occurred to her. "Who wants to buy stocking stuffers, anyway?"

"Don't start with me," she snaps. Case closed.

So it's like that around here.

Consequently, whenever Matt texts me to come over, there's always something going on that gets in the way. I find myself relieved.

CHRISTMAS EVE

My parents both tear up at the sight of me in my Christmas tie and a blazer. I can't wear my good suit anymore, the one I had to wear to the funeral, but there's no viable excuse to avoid the Christmas Eve service. It was Sheila's favorite event of the church year, and we all know it.

They hug me, then usher me to the car. The shit of it is, I want so badly to be a good son. I want to do right by my parents. I want to do right by Sheila's memory. I also need a new way to pretend that the things that are wrong aren't wrong, and maybe closing my eyes during "Joy to the World" will get it done.

The sanctuary is festooned in pine greenery, bright poinsettias, and plastic holly. It's like making the salad, only harder, because there's no one by my side to hear me screaming *arugula* during "Silent Night."

EARTH TO KERMIT

That night, the club sucks me into another raucous online gaming session, for no clear reason. It's epic, as ever, but I'm exhausted.

"I'm soooo stuffed," Janna complains, jamming yet another sugar cookie into her mouth. "I'm gonna have to let out my cheerleading uniform at this rate."

"Stop teasing," Simon counters. "Some of us only have fruit-cake on hand. I'd give anything to sink my teeth into some of that evil white icing. Raaar." He makes a mock-vicious biting face.

"They're so good," Janna says. "I'll bring some over tomorrow."

"Nah." Simon shrugs.

"Please." She puts her face close to the camera. "Take some. Save me from myself."

"This culture is way too thin-obsessed," Celia says. "Eat the cookies. You'll be fine." It's very much something Sheila would have said. It makes me smile and ache at the same time.

"Eat the cookies," Matt whispers in a rhythmic chant. "Eat the cookies."

Patrick joins in, then Celia, then Simon, then me. "EAT THE COOKIES," we chant, and it comes through awkwardly out of synch due to the video chat effect.

"Noooo." Janna covers her ears, with a cookie in each hand. "Okay, fine." She jams another one in. "What would I do without you?" she mumbles, chewing.

"Us?" Matt asks, with faux innocence.

"No, the cookies," she quips. "In fact, you're all cramping our style here. We need to be alone. Peace." She signs off, dropping the squares on the screen down to five. I want to laugh at their joking, but I'm rapidly losing steam. It's a relief when the others begin to sign off over the next few minutes.

Matt video chats me privately after everyone logs off, and I find myself in no mood. "Why are we even having this meeting? What is the point of this?"

"We held it because of you," Matt says. "You seemed like you needed it. That's what we do."

"Me? I didn't ask for that." Maybe I want to be left alone sometimes.

"You're moping around here. You don't even want to hang out. Stuff's going on, clearly."

"It's not that I don't want to," I protest, unsure if it's the whole truth. I crave time with Matt. I wish for his arms around me. But the timbre of his voice is tinged by whatever he's been drinking.

"I'll see you soon," I say.

"Day after tomorrow?" he asks. It'll be a Friday. Our night.

"Of course." The last of my waking energy goes into a smile.

"Hey," he says. "You know I—I'm always here." The pause is significant, like he was going to say something else. Something I can't hear without melting and dripping away entirely, into nothingness.

PICK A LANE

On Friday, Matt is his buoyant self. He picks me up and we play laser tag and the glow of it is perfect, as usual. But then I'm too quiet in the car on the way to his house.

"You doing okay?" he asks.

"I don't know."

"Yeah." He turns the music up. A song we like, with a good beat. We bob our heads to it until we pull into his driveway.

In the basement, Matt's first stop is his liquor stash.

I take his arm. "Could you . . . not?"

"It's just to take the edge off."

"It's only me," I say. "What edge?"

He's annoyed. "This is how I blow off steam. You know that."

"It would be nice if we could just be together and talk. Instead." What I'm craving is stillness and calm, our fingers laced together. I want to say things into the space between us and not worry that he won't remember.

"Fine." He sweeps me into his arms. "Anything for you, sweet Kermit of my heart."

He twirls and dips me like Fred Astaire in a sepia-toned movie. The glow of that fills me with delight.

We lie in the hammock, kissing and goofing until I'm somehow both stirred up and relaxed.

"This is nice," I whisper, running my finger along his jawline. He keeps himself clean-shaven, but it's evening and there's the slightest hint of stubble coming in.

"Yeah," he says. Our legs are entwined and the closeness is thrilling.

"Are the holidays weird for you?" I ask. "It's been weird for me, the first and all."

"The first is a thing," he says. "Maybe it gets easier. Anyway, let's talk about something else." He touches his nose to mine. "Or not talk about anything."

This was only his second year spending Christmas without his mom. *Does* it get better? I genuinely wonder. I can't imagine next year feeling much better.

Matt pushes away—not far, due to the constraints of the hammock, but enough to feel symbolic. "Can we not?" he says, echoing my tone from earlier. Touché.

"I like how sometimes we talk," I say.

"I can't," he says. "So drop it."

Our sweet, cozy bubble has shattered, and I shattered it. Once when I was a child, I picked up a glass vase that I wasn't supposed to ever touch. The temptation was too great and one day I grabbed it. I knew immediately that it was too heavy, that I wouldn't be able to carry it, that I should set it back down, but still I held it and tried to run. The shatter was epic.

I feel it now, that you-should-put-this-down feeling. But reckless desire wins and I can't. I run with it.

"Sometimes at night, you tell me things that matter. I want us to talk, like that."

"When I'm drunk," he says. "It's different."

"Why? Why does it have to be different?" He's inches away; our legs are still touching, but my body and soul cry out like he's left the room, left the building, left the planet.

"So, you want me to not drink, but act like I've been drinking?" He throws up his hands. "Pick a lane, Kermit."

"Can't we be ourselves together? Without it?"

"This is who I am without it," he says, pointing at his torso. "I get why you don't want this guy, but I don't know how to be different."

"I like you how you are," I say. "That's the point."

"Feels like you're asking me to change," he says, and I don't know how to respond to that.

SHARDS

Matt drives me home instead of having me sleep over. I guess this is how it feels to have a fight with your boyfriend. If he even is my boyfriend. I've been thinking about it that way, but we never put a name on it officially. Because there are things we don't say.

The air between us, usually so warm and refreshing, tonight is strangely cool and sharp. I moved the vase I shouldn't have and it shattered.

"Thanks for the ride," I say.

Matt says nothing as I get out of the car.

HYPERSPACE

Days go by with no contact. I ache through it. Should I call him? What would I say? Is it me who needs to apologize, for pushing too hard? Is it him who needs to apologize for refusing to show me his heart? Was it too much to ask?

I don't know. I don't know.

I keep *Star Trek* reruns playing 24-7 and vegetate, imagining myself flying through hyperspace on a starship.

I JUST WANNA FLY

"Heyyyyyy." I recognize the slur in his voice. Can't help but glance at the time in the corner of the phone screen. It's not even one in the afternoon.

"Hey, Matt. What's up?"

"I miss you."

"I miss you, too." *Very much.* The tension between us has been pushing us apart, and I don't know why he thinks calling me drunk is going to fix anything. I crave him and yet it's too painful to keep getting pushed aside. "What do you want?"

Silence. Then light humming in a tune I don't quite recognize. A song my mom likes, I think. An oldie.

"What's going on?" I ask. "Have you been drinking?"

"Just a sip," he says. "Just a nip." He laughs.

Yeah, sounds like it. I sigh. "Are you at home?"

"'Bout to be."

My heart skips painfully. "You're not driving, are you?"

"Nonono. I'm flying." He hums a little louder.

The hair on the back of my neck goes up. I slide to the edge of the couch, all my senses heightened. "What? Where are you?"

"You know," he says. "Where we fly?"

"You're in the park?" That means he drove there, possibly

drunk. And either way, it means he'll have to drive back. Unless he's gone camping without me.

I swallow my disappointment and put Matt on speaker. Pull up my text thread with Patrick, because I know he has a car. This counts as club business, for sure.

> I need a ride ASAP

That sounds a little rude, maybe, so I add,

> Club business

"Okay, well, you need to stay there until I can get there," I tell Matt. "Don't get back in the car, OK?"

"I think I'm going to kill myself," he says into the phone.

My throat fills with phlegm. My heart beats double time. "What?"

Humming.

"What?" It's barely a breath. I have no air.

"I can't do this anymore." The unusual seriousness in his voice radiates. For a moment, he sounds completely sober. "I wanted you to know that I do love you, Kermit."

I slam my feet into my shoes. The phone fumbles and tips in my fingers. "Where are you? For real. In the park?"

Oh God. It all clicks as the image of him sitting at the edge of the cliff fills my mind. Oh God.

"Hmm," he says. "I think it's going to be beautiful."

"What did you do?" I demand. "Tell me."

"Hmm. Gonna do a little flying," he says. "All the way down."

"Matt!" I shout. "Listen to me. Don't move."

I put Matt on speaker again and pull up my text window, find Patrick's thread, and dash the words off quickly:

Emergency

Matt

Pick me up RN

"Where would I go, baby?" Matt says. A beat later, he starts full-on singing. Oldies rock, for sure. "I just wanna fly."

EMERGENCY, WITH A VENGEANCE

I'm on the porch waiting when Patrick pulls up ten minutes later, with Janna in the front seat.

"Drive south," I whisper. "State park."

"Matt, I'm coming, okay? Wait for me."

"Why aren't you here already? I miss you."

"I'll be right there. Don't move." I cover the mouthpiece. "He says he's going to kill himself."

Janna gasps.

"Did you call 911?" Patrick whispers.

I shake my head, pointing at the ongoing call. I'm literally trying to talk Matt off a ledge here. I can't disconnect.

"Jesus, Kermit!" Janna bursts into tears and whips out her cell phone.

RIDE LIKE THE WIND

Patrick guns the engine, making record time along the highway. Janna sobs quietly in the front seat. I'm irrationally angry that Patrick stopped to get her. Her house is right down the street from his, but still. Minutes matter. Seconds, maybe.

"Hurry, goddamn it!" Janna snaps.

"Maybe we'll earn ourselves a police escort," Patrick mutters, letting the speedometer tick upward.

"Talk to me, Matt," I say, trying to keep my voice gentle. It's a fight to hold down the anger and fear that are rising in me. "Keep talking to me."

"What's left to say, Kermit?"

Anything. Everything. A lifetime of things.

"You can tell me anything, Matt. I want to hear about all of it. Talk to me."

"No, you want to escape, just like me."

"I—there are lots of ways to escape that aren't permanent," I say. "We can find more of them."

"Maybe what I want is permanence," he says. "Maybe I want it to be over. No more pain."

I've said the wrong thing, but it's too late to walk it back. I'm no kind of expert in what's happening now.

"We can get through it," I tell him. But I don't know how. I don't know.

"Wait for me," I insist.

Silence.

"Matt, wait for me. We'll go together."

Janna whips her head around and stares at me.

I shrug at her. What am I supposed to say? Wouldn't she say anything to save him, too? "Matt? Matt!"

Strobes of terror. If he jumped, I would know, wouldn't I? I'd hear it? Or he'd say goodbye?

Not everyone has the chance to say goodbye, Sheila says.

"Matt!" I shout. "Talk to me."

Janna presses her hand against her mouth, holding back her sobs. Patrick reaches across the console and grabs her other hand.

"Kerm, you're too beautiful for this world."

"I'm exactly where I'm supposed to be. On my way to you."

"I wanted to tell you I love you. I've never said that to another guy before. Just so you know."

"Wouldn't you rather say it to me in person?"

"It's too late for that."

"Promise me you'll wait. Matt, promise me."

"I can't stand it anymore."

"Yes, you can, goddamn it!" The anger is slipping out. I'm losing control. "You can. You are stronger than any of us."

"Nah, I am the weakest link." He says it, imitating the mechanical voice of the old game show.

"We're almost there," I tell Matt. Patrick whips past the state park entrance and I lean forward to point out the directions. I've been here only a few times but I think I can get us close.

EMPTY

I lose reception on the call near the trailhead. We sprint up the path, leaping rocks and roots, making the journey in record time. We come into the clearing and my heart stops.

I don't see him.

"Matt!" I scream, falling to my knees.

The cliff is empty of all but rocks and grass. Matt's pack and the parachute lie discarded near the lip of the low drop, where we jumped and jumped and always landed safely.

"Oh no," I moan. "Oh God." Patrick puts his hand on my shoulder.

"Here!" Janna shouts. She sits on the four-foot ledge, then launches herself over. "He's here."

I stagger to my feet. Patrick grabs my arm and helps me over the uneven terrain, because all I want to do is run and I keep tripping.

Matt's passed out at the base of the small rock wall. I've never been so happy to see his drunk ass.

Janna pats his cheeks until he wakes, groggy.

"Leave me alone," he moans. "I'm trying to die here."

"Yeah, well, you're fucking it up," she says. "Thank goodness."

We get him sitting up, but he's barely coherent. His eyes are glowing and dilated like tiny solar eclipses.

"I don't think that's just booze," Patrick says. "I wonder if he took something?"

Beside him is a near-empty bottle of his dad's expensive whiskey. Janna digs through his pack and finds an empty bottle of prescription pills with his mom's name on them.

"Shit," Patrick says. "He could've taken those an hour ago."

"Maybe less," Janna says. "He was okay and talking to Kermit until a few minutes ago."

"He wasn't okay," I say.

Janna's tears begin anew. "Yeah, duh. You know what I mean."

"Come on. We can't waste time," Patrick says. "Let's get him up."

It takes all three of us to bring Matt to his feet. Sort of. He can't stand. His eyes are open, but I don't think he's conscious. I'm flushed with rage and terror. We got to him. He didn't jump. And yet it still might not be over.

"I can carry him," Patrick says, half bending, half crouching in front of Matt. "Get him on my back."

Janna and I carefully drape Matt over Patrick, piggyback style. But he can't hold on. We use the parachute like a Baby-björn and wrap them together. Patrick clutches the tarp at his stomach and starts inching toward the trail.

Going down this way is much slower than coming up was. Janna walks ahead and Patrick holds my arm to steady himself. He's a big guy, but a passed-out Matt's not an easy load. Less than halfway down, we meet the paramedics coming up. They get Matt on a stretcher and check his vitals.

Janna shows them the pill bottle. "We don't know how many were left."

The paramedics hump Matt down the hill double time, like it's their usual Saturday jog. I shiver to think maybe it is.

SHAKE IT OFF

Patrick puts his arm around Janna. Now that we've done our part, and Matt's in professional hands, it's time to collapse, apparently. She wails into his shoulder.

"Come on," I say. "We have to go after them."

When we reach the parking lot, the paramedics have Matt on the stretcher at the door of the ambulance. Simon and Celia are huddled by Simon's car.

"Are any of you a sibling?" one paramedic asks. Maybe someone answers.

I'm at Matt's side. They've given him something and he looks more alert. His eyes flick over me. "Hey, you." He stretches up and kisses me on the mouth. In front of everyone.

I wipe my mouth with the back of my hand, then wish I hadn't. Maybe one betrayal deserves another. Or maybe it's because everything that's wrong was in that kiss. I can still taste it.

The paramedics heft him into the back of the ambulance, tearing him away from me. And then they're gone.

"He's going to be okay," Janna says. "Isn't he?" She and Celia are holding hands.

"How did you know where to send them?" I ask Janna, still reeling from the EMS flurry.

"I've been hiking here with him before," she says.

A tearful Celia rushes forward and hugs each of us. "He looked bad."

"Yeah, it's bad," Patrick says.

"So what are we going to do?" Janna says.

Something escapist, I imagine? But no one speaks. No one moves. No one offers an idea for a long, long minute.

"We can't not talk about it," Celia blurts out. "I mean, come on."

"This is an unprecedented situation," Simon mutters.

"Let's get out of the cold," Patrick says. "And then, yeah, we should talk about it."

CARAVAN

Simon had the forethought to ask the paramedics which hospital, so we know where to go. We have three cars now, including Matt's. Janna still has his backpack, which turns out to have his keys, and so Patrick sends the two of us in Matt's car.

It's weird, riding in the seat I've ridden in so many times now, but without him behind the wheel. If I turn my head and look out the window, I can almost pretend—

Janna sniffles.

So much for fantasy.

"It's going to be okay, right?" she asks. "He's going to be okay?"

"He has to be," I answer. "We need him."

CLUB RULES

The room is as cold as the secret. We wait on green-cushioned chairs, in the emergency room lobby. Matt is somewhere inside, in a room or behind a curtain. They won't tell us anything, but they can't make us leave.

We cluster in one corner, Celia and Janna huddled together on a single chair, Patrick leaning against the window and Simon perching on an end table, knee to knee with the girls. Me, an island, hovering across the aisle from them.

"This once, and only this once, we violate club rules," Simon begins. "What the hell just happened?"

"I didn't know it was this bad for him," Patrick says.

"I think I did," I admit. "We went up there one time, and he was talking about jumping. He had this look on his face, but I thought it was—I didn't know what it meant. People say stuff."

"Yeah, they do," Patrick agrees.

"I don't understand," Celia says. "Someone like him. Doing this. I mean, any of the rest of us . . . no offense."

"He's really unhappy," I confess. Why didn't I see it more clearly all along?

"He's the happiest of all of us," Celia protests at the same time that Janna says, "How do you know?"

"Because he showed me. I was just too caught up in my own thing to really see what he was trying to tell me . . ." The ugly green waiting room cushion catches me as my knees buckle. My hands cover my face. "Oh God."

"Kermit's right," Patrick says. "Matt's been faking happy. Haven't we all? The club is bullshit. Not talking about anything is bullshit."

"That's not fair," Celia cries. "We're supposed to help each other. We're supposed to call each other in an emergency."

"He did call," Simon points out. "He called Kermit."

Celia turns away. I know she's crying. Maybe we all should be. Patrick puts his hand on her shoulder.

"We knew and we didn't tell," I say. "That makes it our fault as much as anything." I say "we," but it's me. I should have known.

"That's not fair," Celia says. "How could anyone know he was that close to the edge?"

"I don't know," Patrick says. "How much can we ever know? Even about ourselves."

Everyone goes quiet. We all look at him.

"What?" Patrick says, crossing his arms a little defensively. "Like you never thought about wanting to die? After what's happened to all of you?"

"But, not, like, for real," Celia says.

"How do you tell the difference?" Simon asks. No one knows the answer to that.

"Kermit?" Janna scoots forward, reaching across the gulf that separates us. Her hand presses mine. Out the window, a light snow is falling, the kind that dusts the pavement for a moment, then melts. "On the phone, you told him you'd go with him."

It's embarrassing, her putting my business out there like that, in front of the group. "I was saying anything I could think of to stop him."

"Was it true? Do you feel like you want to hurt yourself?"

"No." But when I said it, I meant it. Reflecting back to that moment, under the panic, under the desperation, there was a feeling of . . . relief. "Maybe."

I'm out of defenses. Janna's wide caring eyes press upon me, and my shields are too damaged to deflect the onslaught. "I don't know if I could stand losing anything else. I don't know if I can stand to hurt anymore."

CLIPBOARD

When the administrator with the clipboard arrives to take our statements, Patrick takes care of all the business—giving them Matt's address and phone number and turning over his bag. We called his home phone, but there was no answer, and none of us have Matt's dad's cell. Presumably the number is locked away somewhere in Matt's phone.

Then parents start arriving. Celia's first. She called them. Apparently, they have that kind of close-knit way about them. Janna's dad comes, too, and he takes over the conversation with the hospital administrator, because someone has to be the grown-up here. There's still no sign of Matt's dad.

It occurs to me, amid the blur of it all, that maybe I should call my own parents. There was probably a time when I would have. But they're fragile right now, and hearing *Please come get me from the hospital* would alarm them. Tack on *I'm not hurt; it's my boyfriend* and they'll completely self-destruct.

I shouldn't think thoughts like "self-destruct" anymore, should I?

Mentally, I try to steel myself for the moment Mr. Rincorn arrives. I imagine him rushing in, wild-eyed, looking to us—to me—to understand what could possibly have happened. And out of nowhere, I'm filled with rage—at Matt. How could he do this?

Matt has a dad who loves and accepts him, even if he's not very . . . present. A dad who's cool with him having a boyfriend and who doesn't force him into lessons about sin or believe he's going to hell. How could he do this to his dad? How could he even think about leaving him all alone?

How could he do this to me?

BEDSIDE

We wait hours, but Matt's dad never shows. No one will tell us where he is, or why. They won't let us see Matt since we're not family, but we can't let that stand. He has to know he's not alone. Now more than ever.

After the others have gone home, dragged from the scene by their parents, Simon distracts the nurses so Patrick and I can slip in to Matt's room in the ER. As we move down the hall, Patrick says, "Would you rather go in alone?"

I would, but I shake my head anyway. "He needs to know we're *all* here."

His bed is by the window, with a curtain between us and the door. The other bed is unoccupied. The light is dim, just a narrow, buzzing strip across the wall above the bed, and the ambient glow from the sunset light outside, through the window.

Matt's wrists are tied to the bed rails with soft restraints. Somehow, that's the sight that causes my eyes to prick. The administrator told Janna's dad there's no psych ward here.

At first I think he's asleep, but then he says, "Kermit?"

"And Patrick." Patrick comes up beside me. He stands at the edge of the bed and squeezes Matt's foot through the light blanket. "This is a stealth visit. We're not supposed to be here, so we only have a minute. But we're all here. The whole club. Anything you need, man. You hear me?"

"Yeah, thanks," Matt says.

Patrick backs away, his eyes on the restraints. He looks as freaked out as I feel. "Anyway, I've got to, uh, go make sure no one saw us. I'll see you. Get well. We need you." And then he's gone. I'm grateful and also not. But I'm in it now.

I perch on the edge of the visitor chair. It's the first moment we've had to ourselves since it happened. He's still groggy a bit, maybe from the meds wearing off. I don't know what they've done to him—pumped his stomach? Flushed his system some-how? Given him an antidote? He's quiet for a while, and I don't have anything to say. Or at least, I don't know where to begin. Maybe I have a lot to say, but I never know how to say it. Maybe that's the whole problem.

"Are we going to break up?" Matt says.

"*That's* what you're worried about right now?"

"I always worry about it."

That's news to me. "You should focus on getting better," I say. "That's all that matters."

"So we are?" he says. "You didn't say no."

I shake my head. "No. I mean, I don't even know how to think about it right now."

"Why would you want to stay with a loser like me?" he mut-ters. "I can't do anything right." The unspoken corollary pisses me off.

My fingers fumble toward his. "Stop. I'm really glad you didn't die. I need you."

"You do?" He looks like a little boy, all tucked in. Holding hands is awkward with his wrists tied to the bed, but I can't let go.

"I don't know how to survive without you."

"Me either," he says. "So what are we going to do?"

"You're going to get better," I tell him. "You're going to come home and we're going to have so many adventures." I don't know if it's true, but it's the right thing to say, probably.

"Are you feeling any better?"

"I don't know," he says, turning his head away. My heart blips. He's in a safe place now, in a place where they won't let him hurt himself, but it all still aches, to know he wanted to. In spite of everything. In spite of *us*.

"You don't feel any different now? Compared to before?" The words slip out of me. Maybe it's wrong to ask. Healing, we know, takes time.

"It didn't feel like anything to me," he says. "I don't feel anything anymore."

PRODIGAL

Patrick drives me home. We're quiet the whole way, but when he pulls into the driveway, he turns the engine off. "Do you want me to come in with you?" he asks.

"No, I can do it." It's only the second-worst conversation I can imagine having with my parents.

He seems uncertain. "You have to tell them, though. For real."

"I know." Putting two feet on the driveway is only the first step.

Patrick rolls the passenger window down as the door closes behind me. "I'm going to text you later to make sure you did."

"Thanks. And, thanks for the ride."

Patrick pounds his fist on the steering wheel. "Glad I could help. And glad we got there in time." His voice cracks.

We look at each other through the open window. There's nothing more to say, but it's one of those moments that hits like a lightning strike. It leaves me with the sense that whenever we look at each other for the rest of our lives, slivers of this exchange will be present.

"You saved his life." I echo his fist pound with one of my own, on the door. "You and your lead foot."

Patrick laughs through his tears, and the sound buoys me for the walk up the flagstones.

BLESS ME, FATHER . . .

Dad's in the den reading. He frowns when he sees me standing awkwardly in the doorway. "Kerm?"

"My friend Matt almost died today," I blurt out.

Dad closes his book and sits up. "What happened?"

"He—" The words won't come. "He—"

"Come here," Dad says, and I do. We sit on the couch and he puts one hand on my shoulder and I lean into him, because if not now, when?

Dad calls for Mom. Gently, so as not to alarm her. All of a sudden, I'm shaking. Speechless. Mom squeezes onto the loveseat. All three of us in a line. "Baby," she says, clutching me. "What happened?"

"Was there an accident?" Dad asks. A fear that is close to the surface, always.

"No, he tried to—" Why can't I say it? That's the whole problem, isn't it? All the things we can't say.

I breathe. Push it all out fast. A version of it, anyway. The cliff, us racing to find him, the ambulance. Without mentioning the club by name. Definitely without mentioning the kiss. "He was depressed and hiding it from everyone."

My eyes are dry, but my whole body is shaking. Dad keeps

his arm around me. "You two seem to be getting close," he says. "That must've been scary."

"Yeah. He's . . . a really, really good friend," I say. "His mom died a while back, so he's been helping me. About Sheila."

The easy thing would be to rest in Dad's arms, but I push away. Mom clings to my arm. It is the hardest thing I've ever had to say, but it's in me, like a rock, and if I don't say it, maybe all of me will become a rock. Maybe I'll start to feel nothing, for real, instead of only pretending. Like Matt.

"I don't want what happened to him to happen to me. I—" I swallow hard. "I mean, don't worry, I'm not—I don't want to—" God, I'm making a mess of this. "Maybe I could use a little bit of help?"

IT'S OKAY TO BE NOT OKAY

The inevitable amount of fussing ensues. Strangely, I don't mind. It's like a dam has broken and I can be myself again. Well, sort of.

Apparently, the self I need to be right now is curled on the loveseat with my head in Mom's lap. She rubs my scalp and it feels good. It feels good, but still I ache. For all the sadness, sure, but also for all the certainty that the next time I have to sit them down for A Big Conversation, it won't end with hugs and affection and tears.

"We'll ask at church," Dad says, regarding my future in some sort of counseling or therapy.

"No," I blurt. It's the closest I might ever come to speaking the truth. "I don't want pastoral counseling." Patrick got these brochures about local mental health resources from the nurses for all of us. I fumble one out of my pocket. "This is a list of places to try."

Dad looks at the brochure like it's more significant than it is that I've been carrying it in my pocket.

"They gave them to all of us at the hospital," I explain.

"I'll look into the options," he says.

WATERWORKS

Finally, they let me go to my room so I can sleep. The one thing I have left. The one thing I'm good at.

But then, suddenly, I'm not good at it. Escape is no longer an option. My body shakes. My eyes sting. I clutch my pillow and try to fight it, but the tears come anyway.

Damn it.

I can't cry for my dead sister, but I can cry for stupid, not-dead Matt. Shame for that engulfs me. The tears fall and I don't even know who I'm crying for now. Matt. Sheila. Me. Or all of us, for how dead and sad and flat and gay we all are.

I wasn't gay, doofus, Sheila sings in my head. *Get your facts straight.* She laughs. *Get it? Straight.*

I'm scared of losing someone else, I admit. What's worse is I feel like I'm losing Sheila all over again. Because Matt is the scaffolding for everything I've built to help me hold on to her. It's tumbling down now. Piece by piece. Bricks and planks and mortar spilling over the edge of the cliff, shattered on the rocks. Irretrievable.

DESIGNATED VISITOR

After school Monday, Patrick takes me back to visit Matt. We've heard nothing from Matt, or his dad, or the hospital, and I'm spinning myself in circles over not knowing. When we arrive, we're surprised to learn that Matt's dad has given permission for me to visit.

The nurse looks displeased. "It's supposed to be only family, but under the circumstances we feel it's appropriate that he have a visitor." Her tone makes it sound anything but appropriate.

I'm embarrassed. If Patrick didn't know something was going on between us already, after the kiss, he for sure knows now. "Sorry," I tell him, uncertain what exactly I'm apologizing for.

"Go see him," he says. "It's cool."

Matt's in a different room now, adjacent to the ER, but the soft white cloth still binds him to the bed rails.

"When are you coming home?"

"I don't know. They won't let me leave but there are no psych beds or something. My dad is paying them to keep me anyway," he says. "He's on a business trip."

Right then, I finally understand how bad it is. What parent doesn't drop everything and rush home when they learn their kid got wasted and tried to jump off a cliff? It's lucky for all of us there weren't more pills left in that bottle.

"I'm sorry," I say.

Matt looks at me accusingly. "I can't believe you ratted me out."

"That, I'm not sorry for."

"No," he says. "Some things are between you and me. You told *everyone*."

"It was an emergency. How was I supposed to come get to you if I didn't call Patrick? I don't have my license."

"You didn't have to call the ambulance," he says. "We could have gone home." Does he mean home, to one of our houses? Or . . .

"They saved your life," I whisper. "I did what I had to do."

DAY 3

"**I need a** ride in a bit," I tell my parents. "I'm going to visit Matt at the hospital."

"It's a school night," Mom says.

I roll my eyes and barely refrain from quipping, *Gee, sorry. Next time I'll make sure my boyfriend attempts suicide on a Friday, not a Sunday.* "Well, now is when he's in the hospital."

My parents exchange a glance. Uh-oh.

"Sit down, sweetie," Mom says, steering me toward the kitchen table.

"What."

"We're not sure you should be spending so much time visiting this boy," Dad says.

This boy. "He's my friend. He almost died." There's no way I'm not seeing him.

Mom and Dad glance at each other.

"And I'm his designated visitor, until his dad comes home."

"It's just that, from what we've heard from some other parents, it sounds like Matt's . . . very troubled."

What's that supposed to mean? "Yeah, hence the hospital stay . . . ?"

"It sounds like he needs more extensive professional help,"

Mom says. "For what he's dealing with. A suicide attempt is very serious."

Duh. "I know."

"You can't be sure of how much influence his . . . worldview is having on you," Mom says.

"It's not his fault that things are messy in my brain right now," I argue. "Why would you think that? It's about Sheila, and a lot of things, probably, I guess."

Not that they're wrong about Matt needing help, but by the looks on their faces I'm not sure what we're really talking about. My stomach clenches.

"You're aware that Matt has some additional struggles going on?" Dad says.

It's hard to keep my voice calm. "What is it, exactly, that you've heard?"

If they exchange that glance one more time . . . I press my hands together, then I press them onto the table and slowly stand up.

They won't even say it. So I do.

"You think spending time with Matt's going to turn me gay?" The irony is palpable. How can they not see it stampeding through the room like the elephant it is?

"Sinful thoughts can be very seductive," Dad says. "They almost lured Matt over a cliff."

I'm still standing here, staring at them. Somehow, I'm still here, though a part of me is fading, fading, fading into nothing.

This is the time. This is the moment. The pitch is flying toward me and all I have to do is swing.

Matt's not making me anything. I was gay before and I still am. Deal with it. Take me or leave me.

But I can't. Because we're not even talking about me yet, we're talking about Matt, and the aversion is written all over their faces.

It's supposed to be different. All the books say so. They're supposed to be accepting in the end. The tiny sliver of hope fades, exactly the way the line of light around a door disappears when the lights go out on the other side.

I can't handle this.

"I'm not going to ditch him because he messed up," I say. The rock that is the core of me grows a little bigger. It presses outward, threatening to burst through my skin and explode me. "That's not what friends do."

WAVES

The walk down the hallway toward the stairs feels longer than it ever has. I should feel relieved. The ambiguity I've been carrying, the question of whether to tell them or not tell them that's been hanging over me, is answered. I can't tell them. Matt was right.

Dad called us "fragile," as if it's clear to all the world that my entire being is suddenly made of glass. Which, admittedly, is not far off from how it feels, stepping away from them right now. If I tell them and it goes the way I expect, if I have to face the rejection and the prayer and the loving concern . . . Shattering.

I can't handle it. Not now. Maybe not ever.

Matt was right about a lot of things. I never thought coming out would be easy, but I thought it would be simple. A switch that flips. A terrifying, shining moment with a clear before and after. But it's none of those things. It's not a door that opens to let me through and closes behind me. It's messy and imperfect.

Some people know about me. Matt. Alex. Patrick, and by extension, probably, the whole club. Sheila. Two anonymous paramedics. Matt's dad. Matt's doctor. A nurse or two.

And some people don't. My teachers. Pastor Ryan and Pastor Carle. Dojang Master Klein. Mom and Dad.

That's how it is for now. The fever dream of mythic, glorious out-ness will have to wait.

My legs carry me up the stairs, past my lonely, quiet room and into Sheila's, which is lonelier and quieter still. I find myself on my knees. "Help me," I whisper. I don't know if it's a call to my sister in the beyond, or a prayer to the God who may have forgotten me. I press my fingers into the carpet and let my cheeks stream with tears and my mind scream out its fears until I'm spent.

AD INFINITUM

There's no closure in the real world. *Eventually you'll find closure*, people say. What they don't tell you is that first you have to open everything up. First you have to look into the face of what you have lost and decide you can live with all that's happened.

The worst part about dragging myself up off Sheila's bedroom floor is knowing it isn't the last time I'll have to lose my shit into the ether.

I don't want closure. I don't want closure. It sounds to me like someday, some mythic door will shut with me on one side and Sheila on the other. I don't want to forget her smile. I don't want to stop hearing her laugh. I want her to scream *shut up, loser* ad infinitum, so I will always hear her voice.

ON THE SLY

I'm resigned to seeing Matt in the after-school window only, when Patrick or Simon or Alex can take me over there. Tonight I manage to stay with him longer by getting Alex to cover for me at Tae Kwon Do.

"Hide in the bathroom," Matt says. "They'll only check once, at the end of visitation, and then you can stay past lights-out."

"Fine." I sit on the gray plastic shower chair and wait.

It's silent for a while, and then it isn't. The nurse's voice is muffled and so is whatever Matt says in response. Then the door clicks shut and he calls my name.

"Come here," he says, scooting sideways in the narrow bed to make room for me. He wants me to lie down with him, but it's too weird. I perch on the edge of the bed, taking his hand, which is still bound to the rail. He frowns with disappointment. "Come here."

He wants you to lie with him, Sheila says, and she doesn't mean go horizontal. And that's when I know that I can't anymore.

"We can't keep pretending that everything is fine." That should be obvious, I guess, considering where we are, but it has to be said.

Matt laces his fingers through mine. "Sure we can. We're great at it."

He has a problem with alcohol, and I have to tell someone. He's not okay, and I can't let it slide any longer. The cliffside might have been the worst of it, but it wasn't a one-time thing.

"Are you still telling them it was a misunderstanding?"

"They're going to make me go to therapy," he says. "Some kind of clinic."

I shrug. "You might not hate it."

"I'll probably hate it a little. But maybe not entirely."

"We can't have you jumping off things," I say, which maybe is in poor taste. "So . . . try not to hate it."

Matt smiles. "I wasn't really going to jump."

"I'm glad." We both know he's lying, or at least I do. Although I guess I can't ever know for sure. Maybe neither of us can, and so pretending is easier.

TRUST FALL

"Untie me," Matt says.

"Yeah, right."

"It's fine," he says. "Really. I'm not going to do anything."

I hesitate, glancing toward the hallway. That sounds like one sure way to get my special visitor status revoked.

"Don't you trust me?" he says. And that's when I realize, I still do. Even though I know he lied when he said he wouldn't really have jumped, he's never lied to me about anything before. It was all right there, out in the open. Everything about him is one big cry for help and I completely missed it.

I reach for the buckles on the restraints, maybe only for selfish reasons. I want his arms around me. I want to pretend everything's okay, for one last minute, before he's whisked away from me for who knows how long and possibly comes back changed.

Maybe it's a test. Of him, of me, of God, of the universe. Because, even as I free him, I know: If Matt lets me down, I'll have nothing.

ENOUGH

We sneak up to the roof of the hospital. "I like it up here," Matt says. "I used to come here sometimes."

Given recent events, I'm not too sure we should be on a rooftop. The side walls are high and I can't see an easy way over, but still. When I do leave, I'll tell the nurse. It's not ratting someone out when you're trying to save their life, right?

Right. I know this. I *know* it.

Matt smiles into the starlight, his face gleaming in the glow of the emergency exit sign. "Music?" he says, and I pump up the volume on my phone. The tiny speakers strain to do Billie Eilish justice. Maybe someone inside will hear it and come to investigate, making it no longer my responsibility to get Matt back in bed where he belongs.

Was this a huge mistake?

Matt reaches for my hand. It's anything but a mistake, the way he pulls me to him. The way we fit, the way we sway.

I can't tell him anything about what's going on at home. If this is our last moment together before Matt has to go away, I want it to be perfect. I relax into his arms and I feel at peace for the first time since . . . well, anyway, for the first time in a while.

"My mom loved music," he says. It will be the last time, for a long time, that he mentions her. Here, under the stars, with our fingers intertwined, both of us feeling more alive than we have ever felt.

"My sister loved to sing. Always kinda off-key and at the top of her voice."

"If they were here, do you know what they'd say?"

I tip my face to the clouds, scan for gaps, counting the sprinkling of stars. "That we have to go on. It's okay to let go. Sadness, missing them, it doesn't have to define us." Except in the ways that it does.

"Eeeeeeeenp." Matt makes a game show buzzer noise. "'None of that maudlin shit."

"What then?"

Matt shakes his head. "Dance par-tay!!!!" He taps my phone screen, changing the music from rich harmonious melodies to upbeat Panic! at the Disco.

We are gay teen boys. One of us is closeted. One of us is (or was, or might have been, or could someday again be) suicidal. And still we find it in us to dance.

We are gay teen boys rising up out of tragedy and pain. To have the world tell it, we *are* our tragedy. We *are* our pain. We are everything that is wrong.

Some days, I almost believe them. Almost.

But then our hands meet. No one in the world understands this feeling. How Matt, even at his lowest, makes me feel high. How our aching hearts only ache because life is worth living, and way down deep we know it. And it hurts. It will always hurt.

Matt pumps his hands to the sky and I imagine life with him and without him. I don't know his pain and he doesn't know mine but every once in a while, through the cracks in our foundation, we see each other true.

He is beautiful. He is flawed. I can't get enough of him and it baffles me that I could ever catch his eye.

The boy I love will carry a parachute to the top of a mountain and somehow float down unharmed. He will ride his bike down a hill not holding the handlebars, his hands raised as if conducting a symphony. He will go to rehab and come back, not changed enough, and go and come back again.

Soon enough I will realize that I fundamentally don't understand why it happens. How someone who embraces living as much as Matt does could ever have wanted to die. It will make me fear our collective minds, so full of twists and turns and lies. It will make me love him more and more.

It will hurt. It already hurts. Everything fucking hurts, and still we are bigger than our tragedy. We are not deviant, we are exultant. We are on top of the world.

We are bigger than our tragedies, all of them. Because there's music. There's Matt's fingers in mine and his laugh in my ear. And there are stars all above and around us.

"How are you?" I ask him.

"What?" He leans closer.

"How are you?" I shout, over the music.

"This minute?" he shouts back. "I'm golden."

It's enough. For tonight, it is enough.

NOT THE LAST DREAM

In the dream, Sheila floats and flares. "How much longer?" she asks. "I'm ready to rest now."

Maybe she's talking to me, maybe not. Regardless, the truth is heavy. "I have to start letting you go, don't I?"

"Nah," she says. "I'll always be with you."

"All the books say—" Great, I sound like Dad. "All the books say I should be letting go."

"Letting go, moving on. It's all a metaphor for something we don't understand," Sheila says.

"Do you understand it now? Where you are?"

Sheila looks off into the distance. "The point is just because I'm stuck here, doesn't mean you have to be. You get to keep going."

"I don't want to go without you." The footsteps I've always tried to walk in are fading in front of my eyes. I had that thought before, but it keeps coming back to me. It keeps aching.

"You'll never be without me, loser."

"Bully."

"Tiny man with big hands!" Sheila's mocking tone carries me back to the day we laughed so hard.

"I forgot that one," I tell her. And even still, I don't quite remember the full context. Who will I become, without her to remind me of the little things?

"Then pick something you'll always remember, dorkopterix."

I roll my eyes. "Don't you have something better to do?"

"Than bother you?" Sheila asks. "Not for a million years."

THREE MONTHS LATER

The room is warmed by our presence and bright as the early spring sunshine. We sit in the art room around the large table in silence. Seven chairs today, instead of six.

Matt ambles in—actually on time for once in his blessed life. He smiles at us, but I know he's mostly smiling at me. He tosses himself into the chair beside me.

"What's good?" he says.

"Same old," Simon answers.

We pull out our pennies, then stare at the door and wait.

Matt toes my foot under the table. I stick out my tongue at him. He purses his lips, blowing a tiny kiss in my direction. What we are is still a secret out in the rest of the world, and in my family, but not in the club. In the club now, things get real. Because sometimes you need someone there with you, and sometimes you need someone to hear you scream.

The six of us are learning how to be there for each other in real ways now. Coming together on the cliffside was only the beginning. Once we decided to tackle our problems together, head-on, we got busy. We all filed complaints and eventually got Richie Corner expelled for bullying. Sometimes, apparently, what getting action requires is Janna's lawyer dad putting in a call to the head of the school board. Now Celia's on a kick to establish a student-led disciplinary committee, because the proof is in the pudding that the powers that be don't always take our needs or our words seriously enough.

We petitioned the city council to put up a guard rail along the stretch where Janna's car slid off the road. We're $175 away from our pledge goal in the Race Against Cancer that we're all running in May, on a team named in memory of Celia's sister and Matt's mom. How does running really help anything? I don't know, but we all agree that taking action feels a lot better than staring into the void.

Matt's fingers dance against my thigh, teasing my senses. "You okay?" he mouths, like he can tell I'm lost in my thoughts.

I'm glad you're not dead, I want to tell him, even when he's driving me wild like this. Especially then.

Millie Caswell pokes her Afro-twisted head into the room. "Hello?"

"Come on in, Millie," Celia says.

THE MINUS-ONE CLUB: RULES

"**I don't need** a support group, thanks," Millie says, pushing the box away.

"Right now, this week?" Janna says. "You don't know what you'll need."

Millie's expression turns haughty. "And you do?" Her gaze flicks to me, as if to say, *you putting up with this white nonsense?*

"We've all been where you are, in our own ways." I look at Matt. "And we're still working through it."

He picks up when I stop. "Sometimes you might want to be around people who know how messed up what you're going through is."

"Or maybe you won't," Simon adds. "Whatever. But for all of us, it helps."

It's the same box of note cards, but one of them is new. We revised it together after Matt's crisis.

MINUS-ONE CLUB RULES

1. Tell no one else about us.
2. We rarely talk about *IT*.
3. But if it needs talked about, we're here.

AUTHOR'S NOTE

The heavy themes explored in this book affect many real people to different degrees: grief, depression, suicide or suicidal ideation, alcohol abuse, and mental health, in addition to broader explorations of identity, attraction, sexuality, faith, and acceptance. For those of us who struggle with or relate to these issues in real life, it is important to remember that there are always (ALWAYS!) people out there who understand what we are going through and are positioned to help and support us.

If you are . . .

Questioning or struggling with your sexuality
Grieving a loss
Feeling down or depressed
Having suicidal thoughts
Worrying about a friend in distress
Wondering how to support your queer peers
Contemplating how to come out to your friends and family
Re-evaluating your faith/beliefs in light of your identity
Being harassed, teased, or bullied
Confused, angry, or scared about the future

YOU ARE NOT ALONE.

Here are some real-life resources that my friends and I have found useful when we have big questions about who we are and how we fit into the world, and whether or not we do. The answer: You fit. You belong. The world needs your presence and your voice, and your people are out there. If you haven't found them yet, keep looking. And keep talking to one another, even when it's scary or it hurts. Especially then.

The Trevor Project is the world's largest suicide prevention and crisis intervention organization for LGBTQ (lesbian, gay, bisexual, transgender, queer, and questioning) young people. They offer crisis counseling, education, advocacy, community, and support.

> **Want to know more?** Visit www.thetrevorproject.org
> **Want to talk?** Call the Trevor Lifeline: 866-488-7386
> **Want to text?** Reach out via TrevorText: Text START to 678678
> **Want to chat?** Go to www.thetrevorproject.org/webchat

Substance Abuse and Mental Health Services Administration (SAMHSA) is a program of the U.S. Department of Health and Human Services which provides myriad resources for teens and families. The samhsa.gov website is extensive, but here are a few things to check out:

- **988 Suicide and Crisis Lifeline:** Simply dial 988 to reach a network of over 200 local crisis response call centers.
- **National Crisis Text Line:** Text "START" to 741741 (within the USA)
- **Worried about your friend?** Try one of these conversation starters: https://www.samhsa.gov/sites/default/files/tay-conversation-starters.pdf

- **Mental health resources for young adults:** https://www.samhsa.gov/young-adults
- **Learn to recognize the signs of mental health issues:** https://www.mentalhealth.gov/talk/young-people
- **KnowBullying mobile app** helps students and parents recognize and respond to bullying. www.samhsa.gov/school-campus-health

American Addiction Centers offers information and resources for people of all ages who are concerned about alcohol use disorders for themselves or their loved ones. www.alcohol.org/teens/

Beloved Arise has a mission to celebrate and empower LGBTQ+ youth of faith. It is a movement to fight for the lives of LGBTQ+ youth, particularly those who have been rejected by their faith communities. Their initial focus has been on Christian youth, with a goal of expanding to interfaith and intersectional work via connections with organizations based in other faith traditions. www.belovedarise.org
- They sponsor Queer Youth of Faith Day: www.belovedarise.org/qyfday

The Gay and Lesbian Alliance Against Defamation (GLAAD) is among the oldest and strongest LGBTQ+ advocacy organizations working for equality in the US today. GLAAD rewrites the script for LGBTQ+ acceptance and tackles tough issues to shape the narrative and provoke dialogue that leads to cultural change. www.glaad.org

GSA Network is a next-generation LGBTQ racial and gender justice organization that empowers and trains queer, trans, and allied youth leaders to advocate, organize, and mobilize an intersectional movement for safer schools and healthier communities. A GSA is a "Genders and Sexualities Alliance," which is often organized as an after-school club. There are thousands of these youth-led organizations already working nationwide, and you can also start one in your school or community. www.gsanetwork.org

The It Gets Better Project is a nonprofit organization with a mission to uplift, empower, and connect lesbian, gay, bisexual, transgender, and queer youth around the globe. www.itgetsbetter.org

PFLAG is a community of allies working to create a caring, just, and affirming world for LGBTQ+ people and those who love them. www.pflag.org

StopBullying.gov provides information from various government agencies on what bullying is, what cyberbullying is, who is at risk, and how you can prevent and respond to bullying. www.stopbullying.gov

Students Against Destructive Decisions (SADD) is a student-led national organization that empowers and mobilizes young people to engage in positive change through leadership and smart decision-making. SADD began as an organization working to prevent drunk driving accidents by educating the public about the dangers of alcohol abuse and has since broadened their mission to encourage students to make safe and responsible choices in many social contexts. They offer programs in vehicle safety, substance abuse prevention, personal health, and more. www.sadd.org

What's Your Grief? is a website that offers articles, resources, and support for people who are grieving or supporting someone who is grieving. www.whatsyourgrief.com

See? There are so many people and organizations around the country that want to be there for you and support you and help you support your friends, too. Sometimes it's scary to reach out, but it's well worth confronting that fear or nervousness to get the help you need.

Good luck, dear reader! You are strong and you will find your way. I'm rooting for you!

WORKS CITED

In the course of this novel, I summarized an article written from an explicitly homophobic religious perspective. I don't recommend reading the real article, as it is quite disturbing and may be triggering to many, but from a research standpoint, the correct and proper thing to do is to cite my source material, so here is the citation:

"Responding to a Teen Child Who Says He's Gay." Focus on the Family. https://www.focusonthefamily.com/family-qa/responding-to-teen-child-who-says-hes-gay/

ACKNOWLEDGMENTS

It is a blessing to have many family members and friends who accept me for who I am and who constantly support me in my work. I feel especially aware of this bounty when working on a project that explores what it looks like when that isn't true, a project which delves into so many sensitive areas of our lives. I'm grateful, as always, to my parents as well as my brother, sister-in-law, nephew, aunts, uncles, and cousins for their enthusiasm and encouragement. I'm delighted every day by my constant writing assistants and accidental editors: my two small orange cats. And I'm fortunate to have a large cast of supporting characters in the form of human friends, too: Thanks to Emily and Katy for their advice and counsel in many areas of my work; to Will, Alice, Lia, and Iris for warmly welcoming me to their dinner table when I'm too busy writing to cook; to Cynthia for sending cheerful gifts; to Karen for listening to me babble awkwardly about what my book is about and to Pär for appreciating my procrastination cookies; to Nicole for probably a hundred thousand texts; to Liz, Jenny, Chris, Kirk, and Willa for many Monday night laughs in the midst of the heartaches; to Amy for sometimes actually answering when I call and for always sounding happy to hear from me; and to Martha for always enjoying my cat pics. Enormous gratitude to my agent Ginger Knowlton and her staff, as and the most towering of all thanks to my editor, Kate Farrell, and the team at Henry Holt Books for Young Readers, who collectively helped turn this story from a manuscript into a book.